MARGERY SHARP
FANFARE FOR TIN TRUMPETS

MARGERY Sharp was born Clara Margery Melita Sharp in 1905 in Wiltshire. She spent some of her childhood in Malta, and on the family's return to England became a pupil at Streatham Hill High School.

She later studied at Bedford College, London, where she claimed her time was devoted 'almost entirely to journalism and campus activities.'

Still living in London, she began her writing career at the age of twenty-one, becoming a contributor of fiction and non-fiction to many of the most notable periodicals of the time in both Britain and America.

In 1938 she married Major Geoffrey Castle, an aeronautical engineer. On the outbreak of World War II, she served as a busy Army Education Lecturer, but continued her own writing both during and long after the conflict. Many of her stories for adults became the basis for Hollywood movie screenplays, in addition to the 'Miss Bianca' children's series, animated by Disney as *The Rescuers* in 1977.

Margery Sharp ultimately wrote 22 novels for adults (not 26, as is sometimes reported), as well as numerous stories and novellas (many of them published only in periodicals) and various works for children. She died in Suffolk in 1991, one year after her husband.

FICTION BY MARGERY SHARP

Novels

Rhododendron Pie (1930)*
Fanfare for Tin Trumpets (1932)*
The Flowering Thorn (1933)
Four Gardens (1935)*
The Nutmeg Tree (1937)
Harlequin House (1939)*
The Stone of Chastity (1940)*
Cluny Brown (1944)
Britannia Mews (1946)
The Foolish Gentlewoman (1948)*
Lise Lillywhite (1951)
The Gipsy in the Parlour (1954)
The Eye of Love (1957)
Something Light (1960)
Martha in Paris (1962)
Martha, Eric and George (1964)
The Sun in Scorpio (1965)
In Pious Memory (1967)
Rosa (1970)
The Innocents (1972)
The Faithful Servants (1975)
Summer Visits (1977)

* published by Furrowed Middlebrow and Dean Street Press

Selected Stories & Novellas

The Nymph and the Nobleman (1932)†
Sophy Cassmajor (1934)†
The Tigress on the Hearth (1955)†
The Lost Chapel Picnic and Other Stories (1973)

† these three shorter works were compiled in the 1941 anthology Three Companion Pieces

Children's Fiction

The Rescuers (1959)
Melisande (1960)
Miss Bianca (1962)
The Turret (1963)
Lost at the Fair (1965)
Miss Bianca in the Salt Mines (1966)
Miss Bianca in the Orient (1970)
Miss Bianca in the Antarctic (1971)
Miss Bianca and the Bridesmaid (1972)
The Children Next Door (1974)
The Magical Cockatoo (1974)
Bernard the Brave (1977)
Bernard Into Battle (1978)

MARGERY SHARP

FANFARE FOR TIN TRUMPETS

With an introduction by
Elizabeth Crawford

DEAN STREET PRESS

To

MR J.H. SHARP

Introduction

'WE CAN only hope that this charming piece of impertinence will be widely read for its fine sympathy with youth in all its shapes', wrote Angela Thirkell (*Times Literary Supplement*, 8 September 1932) of *Fanfare for Tin Trumpets*, Margery Sharp's second novel, in which we follow the fortunes of young Alistair French who, with an inheritance of one hundred pounds, plans to 'live on that for a year, and write'. He thinks 'two full-length novels and about forty short stories' may be possible and he 'might do something for the films, too'. Margery Sharp knew of what she wrote, having determined from an early age to become a self-supporting author. Fortunately, she was to prove rather more successful than Alistair and over a period of about fifty years published twenty-two novels for adults, thirteen stories for children, four plays, two mysteries, and numerous short stories.

Born with, as one interviewer testified, 'wit and a profound common sense', Clara Margery Melita Sharp (1905-1991) was the youngest of the three daughters of John Henry Sharp (1865-1953) and his wife, Clara Ellen (1866-1946). Both parents came from families of Sheffield artisans; romance had flourished, although it was only in 1890 that they married, after John Sharp had moved to London and passed the Civil Service entrance examination as a 2nd division clerk. The education he had received at Sheffield's Brunswick Wesleyan School had enabled him to prevail against the competition, which, for such a desirable position, was fierce. It is to him that *Fanfare for Tin Trumpets* is dedicated. By 1901 John was clerking in the War Office, perhaps in a department dealing with Britain's garrison in Malta, as this might explain why Margery was given the rather exotic third name of 'Melita' (the personification of Malta).

Malta became a reality for the Sharps when from 1912 to 1913 John was seconded to the island, where Margery attended Sliema's Chiswick House High School, a recently founded 'establishment for Protestant young ladies'. Over 50 years later she set part of her novel *Sun in Scorpio* (1965) in sunlit Malta, contrasting it with the dull suburb where 'everything dripped', to which her characters returned. In due course the Sharps arrived back in suburban Streatham, to the house in which her parents were to live for the rest of their lives.

From 1914 to 1923 Margery received a good academic education at Streatham Hill High School (now Streatham and Clapham High School) although family financial difficulties meant she was unable to proceed to university and instead worked for a year as a shorthand-typist in the City of London, 'with a firm that dealt with asphalt'. In an interview (*Daily Independent*, 16 Sept 1937) she is quoted as saying, 'I never regretted that year in business as it gave me a contact with the world of affairs'. However, Margery had not given up hope of university and with an improvement in the Sharps' financial position her former headmistress wrote to the principal of Bedford College, a woman-only college of the University of London, to promote her case, noting 'She has very marked literary ability and when she left school two years ago I was most anxious she should get the benefit of university training'. Margery eventually graduated in 1928 with an Honours degree in French, the subject chosen 'just because she liked going to France'. Indeed, no reader of Margery Sharp can fail to notice her Francophile tendency.

During her time at university Margery began publishing verses and short stories and after graduation was selected to join two other young women on a debating tour of American universities. As a reporter commented, 'Miss Sharp is apparently going to provide the light relief in the debates', quoting her as saying, 'I would rather tell a funny story than talk about statistics'. Articles she wrote from the US for the *Evening Standard* doubtless helped defray the expenses of the coming year, her first as a full-time author.

For, on her return, Margery began earning her living, writing numerous short stories for magazines and a well-received first novel, *Rhododendron Pie* (1930), *Fanfare for Tin Trumpets* (1932) draws on these experiences for, like Margery, young Alistair French has moved from the suburbs to Paddington, although his shared room in the apartment house in 'Bloom Street', 'a shabby thoroughfare' west of the Edgware Road, was decidedly less salubrious than the 'neat and almost severe flat' at 25 Craven Road in which Margery was interviewed by the *Daily Independent*. Her cohabitees may have inspired Margery's depiction of the women students whom Alistair encounters, 'curiously alike, with short hair, fresh complexions, and a tendency to wear brown and orange', their backgrounds so different from those of his fellow residents, who represented 'all types of good, common humanity from a Dickensian bus driver, and a pert little shop girl to garage hands and prizefighters' (*Liverpool Echo*, 14 September 1932).

It is as a playwright that Alistair comes to pin his hopes of fame and, in pursuit of his dream, encounters some of the more raffish elements of the theatrical world. One feels that Margery's amusement at Alistair's efforts could well have had some basis in real life, for she too was looking to write for the stage. Fortunately, she was rather more successful in that sphere, a production of her first play, *Meeting at Night*, reaching the West End in 1934, to be followed by others. Margery never forgot what she laughingly termed 'her early struggles', recalling years later that in those early days she knew that to meet her expenses she had to earn £12 a month (*Books of Today*, August 1946). Art imitated life and in *Fanfare for Tin Trumpets* Alistair reveals to us his careful budget, penny pinching that takes no account of the demands of Love.

Margery continued living in the Paddington flat as her literary career developed, becoming a favourite on both sides of the Atlantic. Her life took a somewhat novelettish turn in April 1938 when she was cited as the co-respondent in the divorce of Geoffrey Lloyd Castle, an aeronautical engineer and, later, author of two works of science fiction. At that time publicity such as this could have been harmful, and she was out of the country when the news broke. Later in the year she spent some months in New York where she and Geoffrey were married, with the actor Robert Morley and Blanche Gregory, Margery's US literary agent and lifelong friend, as witnesses.

During the Second World War, while Geoffrey was on active service, Margery worked in army education, while continuing to publish novels. The couple took a set (B6) in the Albany on Piccadilly, tended by a live-in house-keeper, and from the early 1950s also had a Suffolk home, Observatory Cottage, on Crag Path, Aldeburgh. The writer Ronald Blythe later reminisced, 'I would glance up at its little balcony late of an evening, and there she would be, elegant with her husband Major Castle and a glass of wine beside her, playing chess to the roar of the North Sea, framed in lamplight, secure in her publishers.'

Late in life Margery Sharp, while still producing adult novels, achieved considerable success as a children's author, in 1977 receiving the accolade of the Disney treatment when several stories in her 'Miss Bianca' series formed the basis of the animated film, *The Rescuers*. She ended her days in Aldeburgh, dying on 14 March 1991, just a year after Geoffrey.

Elizabeth Crawford

CHAPTER I

I

"QUIETLY, Alistair," said Aunt Gertrude.

And quietly as a mouse, through all the changing panoply of petticoats, shorts and flannel bags, young Alistair tiptoed past the study door. Aunt Gertrude tiptoed too, and all the female cousins who were so often staying with them: for behind that door old Mr. French was studying Aramaic. At his death, and as a direct result of this pious observance, the linoleum in the passage was practically as good as new, but the great locked book-cases, on the other hand, were unfortunately found to contain no fewer than fifteen hundred sixpenny detective stories. Alone among the relatives Uncle Severus remained unmoved, and after lodging a personal claim for the complete set of *Monday Murders*, 1919-1930, refused to discuss the matter further. In a private conversation with young Alistair, however, he became more expansive, and gave it as his considered opinion that the knowledge of Aramaic (supposing his brother to have had any) would have been as nothing compared with the discovery of an occupation which not only ensured at least six hours' privacy a day, but was moreover practically impossible to discuss with women.

"For your father," said Uncle Severus thoughtfully, "was no fool. At least not altogether. Have you seen this?"

And he held out a small Aramaic grammar, clean and smooth as the day it was bought, and bearing on its flyleaf the neat signature: Gordon A. French, 15 Stanley Avenue, Norbury.

"You see the weakness. He had to introduce the note of realism. He had to bluff himself as well as your Aunt Gertrude. I shouldn't be surprised if for the last year or so he actually thought of himself as an Egyptian scholar.

I can see him telling himself, as he reached for a *Monday Murder*, that relaxation is an essential part of the student's program." Uncle Severus sighed. The discovery of the grammar had depressed him.

At the other end of the dining-table young Alistair sat very still and said nothing. He felt he would like to go on doing this for several days, until his thoughts began to straighten themselves out. Ever since the funeral people had been talking to him, one after the other—aunts, cousins, friends of the family, all in the same key of gloating sympathy. And now Uncle Severus. He wasn't so bad as the rest, and hadn't said anything so far about being grateful: but Alistair wished he would keep quiet all the same. He wanted to think.

He wanted to think first, and very carefully, about his father. He wanted to reverence, to regret; to recollect, one by one, every trait of character, every incident of paternal rigor or benevolence, and build of them a permanent memorial whither he could repair at suitable intervals; and he was being handicapped at every step by an almost complete lack of material. All their lives father and son had been on perfectly good terms, meeting regularly at three meals a day, and occasionally, on light summer evenings, assisting one another to roll the lawn; but Alistair racked his memory in vain for any real communion of souls. Their Sunday evening strolls, for instance, had always left him with a slight but definite feeling of boredom. Outwardly complaisant, he had pined for the more liberal culture of the Free Library; and it now struck him for the first time, in the light of those scandalous book-shelves, that his father too might have been stifling a secret impatience. To one so versed in pan-European crime the conversation of a school-master son might well have seemed a trifle flat, and Alistair remembered, with sudden distinctness, the peculiar alacrity of his father's homeward gait. . . .

"There is also," said Uncle Severus, "the question of your future."

That was the other thing he wanted to think about, and as usual some one was talking to him.

"If you decide to live with your Aunt Gertrude you ought to be able to manage quite comfortably. Assuming, of course, that you stick to your job at St. Cuthbert's." The old man looked at his nephew, and Alistair looked back. He was twenty-one years old, five feet nine inches tall, usually described as a nice-looking boy; and in a voice blurred with excitement he now said huskily:

"How much will I have when it's all settled, sir?"

"About a hundred pounds. Enough to keep you from starving for a year."

Alistair drew a deep breath. It was enough.

"Then I shall leave St. Cuthbert's and take rooms in Town."

Uncle Severus put his hand to his mouth and smoothed the long upper lip.

"Is this a decision of any standing?" he asked.

"Oh, rather," said Alistair happily. "It's what I've always meant to do if I got the chance."

"A hundred pounds doesn't go far."

"But it will keep me for a year—you said so yourself, sir—especially as I shan't have to buy any clothes. And if I could have some of the stuff from here, we could get an unfurnished place for practically nothing."

"*We?*" repeated Uncle Severus, struck by a sudden dark suspicion. . . .

But Alistair met his gaze with cheerful candor.

"Henry Brough's coming, too. He's taking a year's training at one of the London colleges—he wants to get a teaching diploma—and the travelling takes up too much time. We're going to dig together somewhere in Town, and eat out as much as possible. We shall live," finished Alistair, "very simply."

"You will," agreed Uncle Severus. Again his hand went up while he regarded his nephew with mournful wonder. At last he said:

"I don't blame you for wanting to leave St. Cuthbert's. It's a potty little school, and I've always said so. But this rushing up to London—I don't see the point of it. Take a month's holiday by all means—go and spend some of your hundred pounds, enjoy yourself as much as you can. When you've had your fling come back, and I'll get you a job with Clark and Bailey's."

There was a short silence. Then Alistair shifted uneasily in his chair.

"How *awfully* good of you, sir!" he said politely.

The old man grunted.

"H'm. I suppose that means you don't fancy the stationery trade. Well, I've been in it for over forty years, and I can tell you you might do a damned sight worse. Think it over." He pushed back his chair and stood up. They met at the door, Alistair trying to express, by the way he held it open, every possible shade of grateful affection.

"I'm blessed if *I* know what you're after," said Uncle Severus abruptly. He paused, half in and half out of the room, with an odd circular gesture of exasperation. "You want to get away from all this—naturally. Your aunt's a very trying woman. But, my boy, wherever you go, you'll have to do something."

"But I am!" cried Alistair, suddenly finding his tongue. "I'm going to work like hell. That's why I don't want to come into Clark and Bailey's. That's why it's such a marvellous opportunity. I'm going to write . . ."

Uncle Severus stared.

"Oh, my God," said Uncle Severus. "Your poor father over again!"

Words seemed to fail him; he grunted once or twice, and stumped out of the room. The moment he had gone Alistair got his hat and rushed round to see Henry.

II

Henry Brough lived just round the corner, the only son of a chartered accountant and a youth of considerable sober talent. On summer evenings he was generally to be seen at work in the front garden, and here Alistair now found him engaged in cutting the grass.

"Hello, Henry," he called, shouting above the clatter of the mower.

Henry brought his instrument to a standstill and looked up with slow pleasure.

"Hello. I wondered if you'd come round."

The small grey eyes were refreshingly unemotional. On Mr. French's death he had been surprised to feel practically no sorrow, only an additional warmth of affection towards his friend; and in view of the exceptional circumstances had even managed to mention this feeling in so many words. But that was a couple of days ago, and the incident could now be considered closed.

Alistair laid his hand along the flat of the privet, and mixed up with its pleasurable prickings was the thought that he liked old Henry very much indeed. Aloud he said:

"I've just been talking to Uncle Severus. He isn't a bad old bird when you get used to him."

Henry waited.

"There's enough for Aunt Gertrude, anyway. I'm glad about that."

Henry stooped and had a look at the left wheel of his mower.

"You're definitely going to this Training College, aren't you?" asked Alistair irrelevantly.

"That's right. London Teachers'. I shall have to be hunting for digs soon." He straightened his back and looked at his friend over the hedge. "I suppose there's no chance of your coming along too?"

For a moment they stared at each other with rising incitement; for it seemed a very great thing, this moving seven or eight miles within the same city, and they themselves adventurers as daring as any since Whittington.

"London," said Alistair.

The big city, the biggest city in the world, the city to loot. Work so incessant that dawn put out the candle and the black coffee grew cold at one's elbow. And then Fame with her trumpet seeking out the humble lodging, and on her heels reporters from every paper in Fleet Street. With a simple and inevitable gesture Alistair took off his hat and threw it into the Dorothy Perkins.

"That's good," said Henry, interpreting the action as an answer to his inquiry; which in a way it was, "Are you going to get another job?"

"No. Look here, Henry"—in his excitement Alistair tried to lean on the hedge and sank half-way to the shoulder—"I've got a hundred pounds. I'm going to live on that for a year, and write. I can do it for a year, can't I? And I ought to make something, even if it's only an odd guinea or two. Do you remember when that aeroplane came down on the Common and I sent an eye-witness account to the *Daily Mail*? I got ten and six for it, and it was only two hundred words after they'd cut it down. Do you realize, Henry, that if I write only a thousand words a day that's three hundred and sixty-five thousand words—two full-length novels and about forty short stories?"

"Gosh," said Henry.

"I might do something for the films, too. That's what Elstree wants—scenarios. The American stories may be junk, but they do photograph." Alistair paused a moment to visualize himself, an international figure, refusing stupendous sums to go to Hollywood. "You see, you'll be at this training place all day, so I shall have heaps of time to work undisturbed, and then in the evenings we'll patronize the galleries and relax generally."

"In the evenings I expect I shall have to do a good bit of swotting," said Henry, tipping the mower to a convenient angle and beginning to wipe the blades with a piece of rag. When that was done he removed the box, emptied the grass into a basket, and asked Alistair if he were coming in to supper.

"Sure it's all right with your people?" inquired Alistair, much attracted by the idea of avoiding his aunt for another couple of hours.

"Oh, rather. There's a ham," said Henry.

He put on his coat, and the two friends walked up the path side by side, Alistair pausing on the way to retrieve his hat out of the rose-tree. It was getting almost too shabby to wear, especially on the threshold of a new life.

"I think I shall get a black one," he said aloud.

Henry looked round.

"For your father? I thought you said he didn't want mourning?"

"No. To wave good-by with," said Alistair.

CHAPTER II

I

Kimberly Street runs west from the Edgware Road through a district where trousers can be bought on the hire-purchase system and popular panel doctors receive presents of fried fish. Between them its slightly dishevelled shops supply every human need, generally at very low cost, and innumerable show-cards urge the passer-by to Take it Home Tonight, Sell those Old False Teeth for Cash, and Give her a Home to be proud of. Special lines like Air Force boots and broken biscuits thrust themselves on the public attention by means of broadly executed posters, a method also favoured by such ham-and-beef shops as wish to disclaim all connection with the firm opposite. Second-hand book-stalls (stocked chiefly with American magazines) alternate with ladies' outfitters, while next door to the police-station Signor A. Bertorelli makes his world-famous ballet-shoes, receiving lovely ladies in a shop the size of a boot-box. Even in late September jars of yellow lemonade stand outside every sweet-shop, selling freely at a penny a glass, and both the Blue Domes and the Komfy Kinema offer 100 per cent talking attractions. It is also one of the few London thoroughfares in which one can be photographed *en passant* by the wife of a War Hero.

In this resourceful neighbourhood Henry and Alistair came to rest at the end of a hot and hopeless day. They had been inspecting unfurnished apartments since early morning, and with a complete lack of success. Hampstead, Bloomsbury, Chelsea—all the recognized haunts of intelligence—had let them down; and it was the merest accident that they should have been returning from Bayswater by way of Kimberly Street.

"This looks a bit cheaper," said Alistair hopefully. They paused outside a *delicatessen* and stared about them. It seemed a maty sort of district. "Could you get to the college?"

"I should think so," reflected Henry. "There's bound to be a tube station. After all, we can't be more than ten minutes from Marble Arch."

The beautiful words chimed to Alistair like Bow Bells. Ten minutes from Marble Arch! He glanced lovingly up and down the road, and suddenly his eye was caught by the picture of a woman and child framed in a doorway across the way. She sat just inside the shop, taking the air with her baby on her knee, while from a point overhead two great swags of white and yellow bathing sandals were looped back in primitive festoons. The Madonna of the Shoe-shop, thought Alistair; and he wondered whether perhaps after all he should have been an artist.

"I tell you what," said Henry. "Well go down the next turning, and if there's anything to let we'll go and look at it. Nothing could be worse than what we've seen today."

The next turning was Bloom Street, a shabby thorough-fare of tall houses and narrow gardens. It was down-at-heel but quiet; and in the window of Number Fifteen was a small, crooked, printed card. It said: "Large Unfurnished Room to Let."

Three days later, which was a Saturday, they moved in.

II

"Twenty by thirty-two," said Henry, pacing enthusias-tically from wall to wall. "It really is a bargain."

They were paying ten shillings a week, and for another five Mrs. Griffin, a charwoman who happened to live on the floor below, had promised to come in and do for them daily. On the landing outside was a sort of cupboard containing a sink and running water, of which they had the use, and this, together with a small cistern-room, completed the top floor. It was very nice and private.

"As long as there's a tap I don't see that it matters two hoots about a bathroom," said Alistair thoughtfully. "We could even get a length of hose and run it across the passage . . ." He was busy tacking a coloured print of the Primavera over the mantel, and also thinking how like Aunt Gertrude it was to make him take the iron bedsteads. Like nearly everything else, they had come from Stanley Avenue, a method of furnishing that appealed to the pocket rather than to the eye; but of course it was only a matter of a novel or so before he changed all that. . . .

"What do you think of weathered oak?" he asked Henry.

"All right in a kitchen," said Henry, who had really very little taste. He had stopped walking up and down, and now began trying some yellow enamel on a piece of wood. If satisfactory they were going to paint the window-frames.

Alistair drove a final tack into the Primavera and stood back to judge the effect. It was not perfectly straight, and he wondered whether Henry would notice it if he left it.

"Dips down a bit to the right," observed Henry immediately.

With the aid of a screw-driver he pulled out the tacks, and was just starting again when a knock at the door made them both turn round.

"Who on earth—" began Alistair.

"Probably the charwoman. Shall I tell her to come in?"

"Right. Only don't let her start cleaning up until we've got a bit straight."

For some reason Mrs. Griffin had come to be regarded as Henry's peculiar responsibility, a charge which he shouldered with the uneasy pride of the amateur lion-tamer. At the present moment, however, and with Alistair to back him, he felt reasonably bold.

"Come in," he shouted.

The door opened, but not on Mrs. Griffin. Just over the threshold stood a girl with a pink dress and a mop of frizzy hair. She had no hat; she was evidently one of the other tenants, and in a shrill sweet voice she said:

"I'm Winnie Parker. Would you like a cup of tea?"

Alistair put down his hammer, Henry his paintbrush.

"That's awfully good of you," they replied.

The girl looked from one to the other with the sharp, inquiring eyes of the Cockney guttersnipe. In build she seemed scarcely more than an urchin, thin as a reed and light enough to be blown along the pavement like a scrap of paper: but her small pointed face under the frizz of hair was bright with every variety of cosmetic.

"We should like some tea very much indeed," said Alistair, having silenced and consulted Henry in the same glance, "if you're sure it won't be too much trouble."

"No trouble at all," replied the urchin politely. "Me an' Ma's just having ours. I'll bring it up." She hesitated, surveying their domestic arrangements with frank interest, and was apparently about to offer a piece of advice when interrupted by a shrill and aged voice calling up from below.

"Winnie!"

"What d'you want, Ma?" screeched Winnie, with surprising force. She did not, however, make any attempt to move.

"'Ere's Charlie Coe."

"What's *he* want?"

There was an interesting pause, during which Alistair scrutinized the Botticelli and Henry examined his brush for loose hairs.

"'E says," reported the aged tones derisively, "'e says 'e wants to marry and settle down."

"I didn't say nothing of the kind!" It was a new voice, youthful, masculine, and justifiably indignant. Winnie grinned.

"That's Charlie all right. Ma always makes him mad."

Thus formally introduced, Alistair had no scruple in grinning back, but Henry, with perhaps finer delicacy, continued to examine his brush.

"Winnie!"

Winnie filled her lungs for the reply.

"Hello, Charlie! Ma been treating you rough?"

"Come down, won't you?"

"Yer tea's getting stewed," added Ma Parker. "Tell those two young fellers to come down and 'ave a cup with us if they want it."

There was a subdued murmur from Charlie, then Ma again:

"'Ow should *I* know? You ask Winnie, she's been gallivanting after them all day."

"You wicked old liar, Ma!" screamed Winnie unexpectedly. "Good thing Charlie knows you, he might believe half what you say." She turned back to the room, and dropped her voice to a social level. "Why don't you, though? Come down and have a cup with Ma and the boys. They'd be ever so pleased."

Though a little dubious as to the extreme pleasure of one boy at least, there was nothing for it but to accept; and with a tentative straightening of ties they followed Winnie downstairs and into a large but exceedingly well-warmed sitting-room which also contained a bed. It was full of people.

"This is Ma," said their hostess, leading them up to a very old lady in a dirty shawl. (She looked not a day under seventy, and must have been Winnie's grandmother at the very least: but the other was evidently the accepted form of address.) "They've come down for a cup of tea, Ma, and they're fixing the room something lovely."

"Pleased to meet 'em," squeaked Ma Parker, fixing them in turn with a startlingly disreputable old eye.

"This is most awfully good of you," murmured Alistair, drawing closer to his friend. "It—it was most awfully good of Miss Parker to come up."

"Kind?" Old Ma Parker sniffed blastingly. "Winnie, she'd go a sight farther than that after anything in trousers."

"She's got a dirty mind, that's what's the matter with her," explained Winnie, with a complete absence of embarrassment. "Come on and meet some of the boys." She thrust a skinny paw through each elbow and led her willing guests to the side of the room farthest from the fire, where they now made the acquaintance of a stocky, bullet-headed youth in an extremely neat check suit.

"Pleased to meet you," said Charlie Coe.

It was so palpable a lie that both Henry and Alistair felt slightly uncomfortable; but fortunately Winnie noticed their distress and hastened to put matters right.

"Here, don't you take any notice of him," she urged, "he's never been the same since he fell off the organ. Be your age, Charlie, they're the new top floor, and never bitten no one yet."

Thus adjured Mr. Coe relaxed sufficiently to observe that he hadn't caught their names.

"Good reason why," riposted their hostess. "I haven't caught them myself neither."

"French," supplied Alistair.

"An' the rest?"

He hesitated, but fruitlessly.

"Alistair."

"Coo-er!" said Winnie.

It was a curious vocable, admirably adapted to the expression of slightly ironic surprise; and Alistair, who knew no Hottentot, also diagnosed a close approximation to the Hottentot click. He apologized profusely, explaining that neither his godmothers nor his godfathers had consulted him at his baptism.

"Oh, well, no one can help their names," agreed Winnie liberally. "There was a kid at school called Khaki Turner, but that wasn't her fault neither."

With the ease of the experienced hostess she now turned the two strangers over to Charlie Coe and proceeded to pour out tea. Mr. Coe, it turned out, was an authority on cars, and soon Henry was telling him about the various basic defects of his aged motor-cycle. Thus isolated (for rather to his surprise the engineer showed considerable interest) Alistair entered into conversation with a youth in a plum-coloured suiting.

"This seems to be a very convenient neighbourhood," he opened politely.

"Oh yeah?" said the youth.

"Probably not more than twenty minutes from Piccadilly."

"Oh yeah?" said the youth, whose name, although Alistair did not yet know it, was Sidney Mason.

"And amazingly near Kensington Gardens—"

This time Mr. Mason did not even trouble to answer, but moving swiftly across the room assisted Winnie to sugar the tea. Charlie Coe followed him with a glowering look, but stuck gamely to his post; and had not Alistair just then remembered about being a writer he might have felt definitely neglected.

His new profession, however, came gallantly to his aid, and leaning nonchalant against the door he began a dispassionate analysis of the bustling scene. The first point to strike him was the remarkable preponderance of males. At the mild Norbury tea-parties on which he had been reared it was extremely rare to find more than four or five men in a gathering of ten to sixteen females; and of these one was invariably either the husband or father of the hostess. But in the present assembly he counted no less than seven single gentlemen (how he knew they were all angle he could not say: somehow they had that appearance) while the feminine element was represented only by Winnie Parker and the old lady. There was Charlie Coe, himself and Henry, the objectionable Mr. Mason, a tall and strikingly handsome youth in spectacles, a boy who looked like the beginnings of a boxer, and finally, seated in the place of honour on one side of the fire, an extremely dignified gentleman with a walrus mustache. With the exception of Ma Parker he was probably at least twice as old as any other person in the room, and all addressed him with great respect. His name was Mr. Hickey.

Faced by such luxuriance of raw material, Alistair almost relapsed into desultory musing; but with a considerable effort he pulled himself together and began seriously to examine the Laws governing Male Incidence at Female Tea-fights. By way of clearing the ground he at once ruled out himself and Henry as being purely fortuitous factors (though it was noteworthy that he had never seen two completely strange young men drop in at Norbury). That left only five, a ratio of two and a half to one; and the moral of *that* was—

Alistair pulled himself up, startled back to sense by an echo from his childhood.

"Here, have a cup of tea," said Winnie.

It was a full-sized breakfast cup, to accommodate which Charlie Coe now drew up a chintz-covered card-table. He also procured two more cups for himself and Henry, and a plate of cut cake. It was studded with large succulent cherries, and each slice would have fed Alistair for one day.

"Your health," said Charlie Coe.

They clinked crockery and drank to their better acquaintance in draughts of strong sweet tea. Alistair meditated a neat epigram on these appropriate qualities, but before he could formulate it Winnie had returned, and was once more at liberty for general conversation. Gracefully accepting the arm of Charlie's chair, and fixing her round blue eyes on Alistair, she at once took up her duty of making him feel at home.

"That's Reg Bennett," she began methodically, backward-jerking at the spectacled Adonis. "He's a commissionaire at the Komfy Kinema. It's ever such bad pay really, but he gets lots of tickets and takes all his friends. Only they won't let him wear his glasses because it doesn't look military, so if ever he doesn't recognize you you'll know why. He's ever such a nice boy." She dug Charlie sharply in the ribs. "Isn't he, Charlie?"

"Might be worse," conceded Mr. Coe. It was clear that extreme good looks of a South American type made little appeal to him; but Winnie appeared to be satisfied.

"That little squit in the purple suit is Sidney Mason. He serves in Sammy's Sandwich Bar, just as you turn into the Edgware Road. I expect you'll see him there one of these days. He makes crab salads ever so nice, with little black things all round the edge. But the boys don't like him much, they say he daren't eat pork, and borrows something awful. Eddie Cribb—him with the broken nose—he looks after a paper stall on the Underground, but he's mad to be a boxer. He'll fight any one for half a crown, or less if it's that or nothing. He says he's related a long way back to the greatest English boxer that ever lived, but I don't know if it's true."

She paused for breath, and Alistair, rather to show his continued interest than because there was any need for encouragement, inquired the name of the gentleman by the fire.

"That's Mr. Hickey," said Winnie. She spoke with that deep reverence usually reserved for Primates and successful financiers. "He drives one of the General 'buses. He's very well off." Respect, it appeared, prevented her from detailing any more human traits, but they all took a good look at him and felt the better for it. For there, majestic in flesh and blood, sat one of the pillars of society: one saw at a glance that he voted Conservative, wore natural wool underwear, enjoyed a friendly pint: and well for society were all its pillars of equal girth and foundation.

"It must be very exacting work," said Alistair respectfully.

"Ooh, it *is*. It's ever such a strain. Mr. Hickey says you wouldn't believe, till you've driven a 15, what fools people are. He says the women are something fierce. Come on, Charlie, lend a hand."

Without any warning she slipped from her perch and began collecting the cups. As at a given signal conversation at once ceased and everybody (except of course Ma and Mr. Hickey) followed suit. Inside five minutes all crockery was stacked in a kitchen-cupboard corresponding to the one on the floor above, and Winnie, girt in a green rubber apron, had begun to wash up. Such was the competition for dish-cloths that Alistair had to go halves in one with Reggie Bennett, but even so they managed to dry at least half a dozen cups between them. By raising the voice it was quite easy to exchange jokes and back-chat above the clatter, no one seemed to drop anything (or if they did, nothing broke), and the fun was at its height when from the head of the stairs came a sound of clapping. It had, however, that quality which distinguishes the clapping of hands in the schoolroom from the clapping of hands in the theatre: it demanded silence.

And silent they all were, Winnie, the boys, even the cause of the interruption himself, who, though apparently trembling on the verge of speech, continued to stand there mutely glaring. He was a tall and sandy youth with the violent countenance of the born agitator, and having obtained his silence seemed uncertain how to use it.

"Hello, Arnold," said Winnie at last. "Come up for a cup of tea?"

Arnold found his tongue.

"I've come up to ask you not to make such a hell of a row," he said loudly. "I've got a meeting in my room, and we can't hardly hear ourselves think."

"Here, you keep your language downstairs," said Charlie. Nonchalant as a couple of sheepdogs, he and Eddie Cribb began to move towards the staircase; but Winnie was quicker.

"Now then, we don't want no rough-housing up here," she cried, pushing her way out from the cupboard. "Come off it, both of you." And leaning over the banisters (for Arnold was now half-way down the flight) she added: "I'm ever so sorry, Arnold, truly I am. But we'll be back in the room in a minute, and then you won't hear a thing." Behind her back Charlie and Eddie groaned aloud, but Winnie merely kicked out at their shins and continued her cajolery. "It's only the washing-up that makes such a racket, and that's all finished. Here, would your meeting like a bit of cherry cake?"

Though barely audible, Arnold's reply seemed to indicate that the apology would pass, and without stopping for further parley he at once continued his way downstairs.

"'Twouldn't have been more than one good clout, anyway," said Eddie, looking longingly nevertheless after his receding back. "He's got no more muscle than a piece of 'am."

"And that's more than you've got manners," said Winnie sharply. "Here, open the door for the tray, will you, and we'll all have a game of rummy. You'll play, won't you?"

Henry and Alistair, thus suddenly addressed, hesitated politely; but after such very large slabs of cherry cake it seemed churlish indeed to refuse, and both were soon happily absorbed in the acquisition of twos. Mechanic and *litterateur*, schoolmaster and commissionaire, all were levelled and united in the glorious uncertainties of the game. Or if there were a distinction, it was that the mechanic and the commissionaire were slightly the better players.

III

From her warm corner by the fire old Ma Parker watched the proceedings with bright complacent eyes. She was not allowed to play herself, owing to an ineradicable habit of cheating, but even so she liked these social evenings even better than the pictures. They warmed her up, put some life into her, and every time Winnie screamed it was as though the cold shadow of the grave receded a degree. At the other end of the table she could see Charlie Coe's bullet head black against the light as he bent over his cards: a good lad, a steady lad, and Winnie might do a lot worse in the end. But there was no hurry. Not when you were young. That was the time to take your fun and kiss your lad and come home with the bracken in your hair. Not that she'd say such a thing to Winnie, of course. Winnie was a good girl. "You're a wicked old woman, Ma!"—that's what Winnie said. Old Ma Parker's throat contracted in a noiseless chuckle. It was odd how, as she grew older, the pleasure parties of her country youth began to return with increasing clarity, so that sometimes she went about a whole day with the smell of hay in her nostrils. . . . New hay prickling up against your neck, and the moon through the barn door. There were too many lights in a town, lights and policemen and magistrates and missionaries. . . . With a sigh of regret for both the happy and ignominious past, she returned to the group round the card table. That was better, that was alive and warm and eager, even if it were only bits of pasteboard they were all so busy about . . . and what went on under the table was nobody's business. . . .

A string worked in old Ma Parker's throat. She wanted to tell them that now was their time, now was their hour to kiss and clip and take their pleasure. For nothing else mattered, only youth. She wanted to tell them that youth is the bright bird of Troy, and Time the plucker; that golden lads come to dust, that in delay there lies no plenty; but the words would not come, and instead she produced only an unseemly hawking noise such as sometimes afflicts the very old.

"Spit it in the fire, Ma," said Winnie kindly.

CHAPTER III

I

THE rich geography of an apartment house in Bloom Street is not mastered in a day, and nearly three weeks elapsed before Henry and Alistair had completed their mental survey. The floor immediately below their own was divided into three rooms, of which two, including the largest, were occupied by Ma and Winnie Parker. In spite of their difference in age, the old woman and her granddaughter lived on terms of remarkable cordiality, a happy state of affairs due partly to Winnie's invincible hilarity and partly to the reduction of all cinema prices before half-past one. This enlightened policy—enabling the leisured but impecunious to get in for sixpence—was the great turning-point in Ma Parker's life. On Tuesdays and Thursdays she patronized the Blue Domes, on Wednesdays and Fridays the Komfy; and since her granddaughter frequently saw the same program in the evening, they were never at a loss for topics of conversation.

Some such occupation was very necessary to the old woman, for Winnie was out of the house by half-past eight and did not return till half-past six. She worked in a drapery shop at the other end of Kimberly Street, a small but enterprising establishment where a lady could purchase every article of clothing from the skin up. It made her rather tired, standing all day, but the actual serving Winnie enjoyed very much indeed. She liked to give advice, to enter into long discussions with all the customers, particularly if they were about her own age, and so distinguished herself in the sale of artificial flowers that they had come to be regarded as Miss Parker's special department. The secret of her success with cotton roses was twofold: she did honestly think them extremely beautiful, and she was also certain that the dance dresses which they were to adorn would look extremely beautiful too. As a result hardly a day went by but some young lady came in with a pattern of jade-green lace; and then Winnie would ransack the boxes and half-empty the window in a search for the exact shade of nasturtium that would bring out its full beauty. No trouble was too much for her: a word from her customer, and she would throw over the whole range of yellows and begin again on pink: at least a quarter of her time was spent on the doorstep matching colours by daylight. At six o'clock, however, she was beginning to feel slightly exhausted, and it was a great relief to get home and be sure of finding the old lady quite bright and cheerful.

"Two shilling a week it costs you," Charlie once reminded her.

"And dirt cheap at that," said Winnie. "Poor old bird, it's the only pleasure she's got."

Old age, indeed, had transformed Ma into the perfect film fan, following with unwearied interest the trials and triumphs of half a dozen stars. Her favourite was perhaps

Adolphe Menjou, to whom she frequently alluded as a proper bad lot: among the ladies, so long as they wore markedly expensive clothes in compromising situations, she made less distinction, and would often try to educate her grandchild out of a passion for Greta Garbo.

("Pretty—she's no more pretty than you are," Alistair once heard her say. "'Air that wants cutting, and about as much curl as a ruler."

"You're behind the times, that's what you are," replied Winnie, busily cold-creaming her face: for the conversation was taking place, like so many others, at about half-past eleven on the third-floor landing. "I think she's just lovely. Coo, don't I wish I looked like that!"

Old Ma Parker sniffed.

"'Olds 'erself like a sack of potatoes," she elaborated. "You'd think she'd be able to buy a pair of stays out of all them 'undreds a week.")

The third room on the Parker floor was occupied by the charwoman who was to do for Henry and Alistair, but this was far less convenient than it looked. Mrs. Griffin liked to have a little work under her own roof, so to speak, and would pop up at all hours to polish the kettle or make the beds. (Alistair and Henry were naturally unable to foresee this disadvantage, but after a week or so were forced to say they would make their beds themselves. For she never seemed to lose the hope that they might be going to stay out all night, and therefore invariably left this essential office to the last possible moment, accompanying them upstairs on their return from the pictures and gratefully participating in a cup of tea.) An aged starling as to personal appearance, Mrs. Griffin also possessed in an unusual degree the acquisitive instincts of all proper charwomen, and seldom came home without a large bundle of things her ladies didn't want. When invited to inspect this booty—she was no miser, and gave freely of her store—Alistair was constantly surprised at the number of perfectly sound walking shoes thus discarded. Ladies who employed charwomen, he sometimes thought, must be very fastidious about their feet.

Mrs. Griffin's apartment being as it were the only foreign concession in otherwise purely Parker territory, Winnie had long cherished a dream of transplanting her elsewhere and renting it for the use of Ma. A dream, however, the project was likely to remain, for the rent—six shillings a week—was prohibitive, even with her money and Ma's pension; besides which, the old lady did genuinely prefer sleeping in the sitting-room. She found it nice and warm.

"One of these days, of course," Henry used to prophesy, "she'll be found asphyxiated, and I shouldn't like to be in Winnie's shoes at the inquest. That tobacco of Mr. Hickey's would do the trick to start with."

But old Ma Parker had been reared in a Buckingham-shire cottage where the children slept three to a bed, and what she suffered from Mr. Hickey's pipe was as nothing compared with what Mr. Hickey suffered from her unnatur-ally powerful snoring.

He occupied the first-floor front, directly beneath her bedroom, and had also obtained virtual possession of the back by coming out and glaring at all prospective tenants. He was done for not by Mrs. Griffin, but by a widowed cousin from the next road, and lived in great ease and plenty on his princely earnings. A lodger of such impeccable standing, it was felt, lifted Number Fifteen well above the common run of Bloom Street; and if he inclined to keep his distance, no one blamed him in the least. Once or twice a week a friend from the Depot would stump heavily up the stairs, and presently a doubled stumping would announce that they had both gone out to the Cock and the Bottle: but as a rule Mr. Hickey's free evenings were spent in the solid pleasures of sleep.

By comparison with this dignified isolation the ground-floor was populous as a warren, though not nearly so animated. In the largest of its three rooms a mother and two elderly daughters kept themselves to themselves and made artificial flowers. They never spoke to any one, and were believed to have come down in the world. Directly opposite lived a very old man called Mr. Puncher, whom Alistair saw every time he went into the Free Library. Here Mr. Puncher apparently spent the day in meditation: but in the evenings he took a tin whistle and went out to entertain pit and gallery queues. (Winnie, with her usual enterprise, once tried to take lessons from him on this handy instrument, but the shock was too great for the old gentleman, and she had to be restrained.)

The third apartment was inhabited by Arnold Comstock.

Alistair's first impression of him, standing white and agitated at the head of the stairs, had been of a tall, overgrown youth of about his own age: but on closer inspection Mr. Comstock turned out to be at least thirty. This air of juvenility was due not to any boyish freshness in his narrow countenance, but to its extreme weakness, a weakness which was reflected in the feeble violence of his speech. He did, however, retain some of the less engaging characteristics of adolescence, being very much freckled, bony about the wrists, and passionately addicted to joining societies. Inevitably a Communist (he held, precariously, an ill-paid post with a firm of box-manufacturers), Arnold Comstock was also a prominent member of the Anti-Religion Society, the Society for Ethical Discussion, and several more of the same feather. In the activities of these bodies he found his sole recreation, and was never tired of listening to the denunciation of capital; but should the meeting, as was not impossible, end in a free fight, Arnold was never known to receive an injury.

"He runs like a rabbit," said Charlie Coe, from whom Alistair received most of this information. "I don't hold with Reds myself, but they'll mostly throw a chair before they bolt. Arnold, he just bolts."

Alistair liked young Charlie. Among all the changing rabble of Winnie's boys he stood easily preeminent, earning very good money in a local garage, and harboring no foolish doubts of his own capacity. Towards his many rivals, as indeed towards Winnie herself, his attitude was one of benevolent tolerance; but he never let a day go by without calling at Bloom Street.

"All this talk about women wanting variety," he confided to Alistair, "I don't believe in it. Girls like the chaps they are used to, that's what I say."

They frequently dined together at the Riviera Café, a small but extremely popular eating-house at the corner of Bloom Street. Apart from a one-and-sixpenny dinner said to be the best value in North-West London, the Riviera was famous for its mural decorations, for the proprietor, rarely conscientious, had had the interior frescoed with a rich *trompe-l'oeil* seascape of waves and clouds. In the immediate foreground, moreover, was painted a life-size balustrade, lavishly festooned with pink roses, in contemplation of which ingenuous customers might fancy themselves seated on some Southern loggia. This stonework was also a source of many happy pleasantries among the regular patrons, who often threatened to commit suicide from its parapet, and who did actually inscribe their twined initials all round the coping. It was an intimate little place, very popular with the inhabitants of Number Fifteen, who were frequently to be seen taking their evening meal and exchanging badinage at its marble tables. Alistair was soon dropping in regularly every evening, but Henry, as time went on, came less and less often, and in reply to his friend's inquiries alleged that he preferred French cooking.

It began to strike Alistair (and not in view of this statement alone) that one could never be said to know a person without having actually lived with him. For ten years he and Henry had grown side by side with Shakespearean closeness, banded together in hoops of classic steel; but three weeks in Bloom Street had already brought to light a number of wholly unexpected traits.

The matter of cigarettes, for example. If ever a man had "Goldflake" written all over him, that man was Henry: yet he now revealed himself as an habitual smoker of caporal. Innumerable butcher-blue packets littered the room: the dark, loose tobacco came out in Alistair's mouth whenever he reached to the wrong box: and his annoyance was crowned when Henry, politely questioned, replied that he had smoked Paquet Bleu for the last three years.

"I never noticed it," said Alistair rather crossly; the implication being that one thinks twice before sharing a room with a man who smokes foreign tobacco.

"Oh, well, you're not very observant," said Henry, opening a fresh packet. "I used to think writers had to notice everything. . . ."

Such breezes, however, were rare enough to act as landmarks, and in general life at Number Fifteen flowed on very agreeably within the necessarily restrictive limits of two pounds a week. But Alistair was quite happy, and never had the least trouble with his accounts. They were extremely simple, and consisted of four main items:

	s.	*d.*
Rent (half) . . .	5	0
Mrs. Griffin (half)	2	6
Food:		
Breakfast, 6*d.* x 7 .	3	6
Lunch, 8*d.* x 7 . .	4	8
Dinner, 1*s.* 6*d.* x 7 . .	. 10	6
Light and heat . . .	. 4	0
	£1 10	2

He also made himself a weekly allowance of five shillings for cigarettes, stationery, amusements, shoe-repairs, razor-blades, laundry, toothpaste, hospitality and 'bus fares; and having thus cut his coat to his cloth, wore it in great content.

The only thing he had not allowed for (and this in an author must surely be considered strange) was Love.

CHAPTER IV

I

WITH the rising of the wind the four fountains at the head of the Serpentine bowed all together in the same direction, like Hans Andersen princesses, spattering the flags with four patches of spray. Behind their falling water the stone balustrade seemed to quiver in the October sun, and behind the sunshine hung a sky so remarkably blue that Miss Tibbald was at once reminded of Italy.

"Quite like Rome," observed Miss Tibbald happily.

She had, of course, only a novel-reader's acquaintance with that beautiful city, but thanks to the circulating library there were few parts of the world in which she would not have felt immediately at home. This vicarious globe-trotting made her a very interesting conversationalist, often surprising strangers by a casual reference to the Sudan; and indeed, before the War put a stop to everything, she had frequently been to Dieppe.

Just beyond the first fountain a girl in a yellow coat stopped to look at the ducks, and Miss Tibbald was charmed by the patch of colour. It made her think of a picture that used to hang in the drawing-room, a picture of a lady sitting pensive on the shores of a lake, with Chinese lanterns in the trees overhead.

"Reflections," it was called: a double meaning. There was a piece of music, too, by a Frenchman, which had always seemed to her very beautiful—*"Reflets dans l'eau."* Miss Tibbald said the words aloud, enjoying her accent, for she had never known any of that dreadful British shyness about speaking foreign languages.

The young man at the other end of the seat looked up in surprise. How odd, she thought, if he should turn out to be a Frenchman, a young student alone in London, and hearing for the first time the friendly accents of his beloved Paris! She looked again, and there on the bench between them lay a soft black hat. It seemed so like a sign that Miss Tibbald took her courage in both hands and leant towards him.

"Quelle heure est-il, s'il vous plait?"

"Trois heures moins quart," replied Alistair politely. His watch was generally a trifle fast, but there was no need to go into that now.

Highly delighted with the success of her ruse, Miss Tibbald next waved a hand at the scene before them and remarked comprehensively:

"Versailles."

Alistair nodded. He was thinking what a superb character she would make for his novel, a little old Frenchwoman living alone in London, and remembering by the Serpentine the glories of Louis Quatorze. Had she come over as a lady'smaid—trim, pert, raven-haired—or the happy bride of some dashing young sergeant? Hastily he ransacked history for a suitable war in which to bring them together; but 1914 was too recent, and South Africa unlikely to have involved many Frenchwomen; so he was just about to fall back on the first theory when a large black retriever, illegally damp, came bouncing towards them. Directly opposite their seat he stopped to shake himself, thus causing Miss Tibbald to exclaim in alarm.

"Oh, you bad dog!" she cried reprovingly.

A slow crimson began to burn in Alistair's cheek.

"Quel méchant chien!" added Miss Tibbald.

"This must be stopped," thought Alistair. "This must be stopped at once." So he said politely:

"I hope you're not very wet?" and immediately began throwing sticks to the *chien* while she recovered from her embarrassment.

The manoeuvre, as it happened, was quite unnecessary. In the flicker of an eyelash Miss Tibbald had picked up the situation, looked at it all round, and decided on obliteration. Without the least pause she said:

"Not at all, thank you. So pleasant here, is it not? I often come and sit for a little in the afternoon. *Ah, les beaux jours d'automne!"*

Alistair looked at her with new respect. That last phrase was a masterpiece, implying as it did that she often dropped into French, whatever the nationality of her companion; and from this it was but a step to the assumption that she had known him to be English all along. He marvelled, wholeheartedly; and even as he did so Miss Tibbald furnished a yet more staggering proof of her mental calibre by saying:

"You write, of course?"

Alistair nodded, too overcome to speak.

"Poetry, or prose?"

"Prose," said Alistair: adding, after a moment's thought, "as yet." Then his curiosity got the better of him, and he asked point-blank how she had known.

"By your hat," said Miss Tibbald simply. (It was quite true, even though she had at first connected it only with France.) "I know a great many writers, and they all wear hats like that."

He looked at her with astonished envy. A *great* many ...

"You must," he said, "have some very interesting acquaintances."

"Indeed I have," agreed Miss Tibbald. "Mr. Barclay, the poet, is a great friend of mine, and many others as well. You see, I belong to a small literary club, which meets once a week, every Friday, and it brings us all together." She paused, considering him from her bright little eyes. "You ought to join yourself, you know. It's called the Embryo Club, and was founded especially to help young writers. I'm sure you'd make many nice friends."

He could hardly credit his ears. Thus to be introduced, at the very outset of his career, into the very *milieu* he most yearned after! The young writers, the coming talents, the men of tomorrow!

"I could quite easily," Miss Tibbald was saying, "put you up for temporary membership. That means you can come to one meeting and see what it's like. Next Friday we have Henry Montague speaking on Youth and Opportunity."

"Henry Montague, who's just written *Epic Death*?" asked Alistair, considerably impressed; for the novelist was admitted to be a great man even by the newspapers.

"That's right. I haven't read it yet, but it's on my list. Should you like to come and hear him?"

Gathering, from the general incoherence of his reply, that he would, Miss Tibbald bade him write down an address to which she might send a card; and it was at this moment that Alistair was suddenly overcome by an impulse of pure altruism. With infinite diffidence he asked if he might bring a friend.

"He's a student of London University, who shares my rooms. He doesn't write himself, of course, but I'm sure he'd be awfully interested."

"But of *course* bring him," cried Miss Tibbald. "It's no bother at all. I'll just send two cards, and you can fill them in yourselves."

"My name, by the way," said Alistair, a little awkwardly, "is French. Alistair French."

"And mine is Tibbald." A faint shadow passed over her face as she watched him note it in his pocketbook. "It's really spelt The-o-bald, you know, but if I write it like that people will pronounce it like that, which is quite wrong. It just shows how standards get lowered."

Alistair tore out the page with his address, which she tucked into a large leather bag; and observing her to be making preparations for departure, offered his escort as far as the gate.

It was accepted with pleasure, and they covered the short distance so quickly and agreeably that he insisted on conducting her across the road to the Tube. Here Miss Tibbald said, *"Au revoir!"* and Alistair, rather ambitiously, *"Jusqu' à jeudi!"* It ought to have been *vendredi*, but they were both too pleased with themselves to notice; and with a final pressure of the hand she disappeared into the station. Alistair stood a moment longer watching her buy her ticket and marvelling at the deceptive appearance of women. For who, faced with that shabby black coat, that pleasant but spinsterish countenance, would have suspected a direct descendant of the *salonnières*?

As soon as she had disappeared Alistair hastened to the Free Library to look up Mr. Barclay in *Who's Who*. Not finding him there, he narrowed the field to *Who's Who in Literature*: but Mr. Barclay was not there either, from which Alistair concluded that he must be very advanced indeed. The book, however, so fascinated him that he sat down beside Mr. Puncher and read it steadily for the next two hours.

II

Returning to Bloom Street just after seven, he was surprised by the apparition of a fashionable young lady on the doorstep of Number Fifteen. A closer inspection showed it to be none other than Winnie, ingeniously attired in a long pale frock and the jacket of her coat and skirt.

"Hello," said Alistair. "I thought you were Tallulah Bankhead."

Winnie looked down at her flowing skirts and preened complacently.

"Not half bad, is it? I got the idea from a shop in Oxford Street. They had a whole window full of little coats just this shape, some of them up to six quid. Fur and velvet, o' course, but then, they've got to give you something for the money." She showed no disposition to hurry away, but stood swinging one foot idly from the bottom step. It was slippered in black, with a prodigiously high, bejewelled heel.

"Saucy, aren't they?" said Winnie. "Mrs. Griffin gave them. Her lady didn't want them any more."

"Saucy is the word," affirmed Alistair. "Who's the lucky fellow tonight?"

"Eddie. He's taking me to the gala night at his Club."

Alistair's mind jumped back to that first Saturday night when they had all played rummy.

"The young man with the broken nose?"

"That's him. Eddie Cribb. He broke it fighting—it was boxing really but he always calls it fighting, because he says this bloke he's descended from was a fighter first and a boxer second." Winnie paused, apparently in deep thought. "You know, it's funny, but when a boy believes in himself like that it's kind of catching. He says in another five years he'll be British Heavyweight, and from then on that'll be World as well." She broke off again, to glance down the road: it was obviously annoying to be kept waiting, even by a future world-beater.

"Has he had any training?" asked Alistair, deeply interested.

"Not like a pro., of course, but a good bit here and there. There was a scoutmaster taught him some when he was a kid, and afterwards that Church in Kimberly Street had evening classes—Eddie, he'd go anywhere for a fight. And fit! He keeps himself as hard as nails. This is the last night out he'll have for ever so." Her voice trembled on the verge of great revelations. She decided to throw caution to the wind. "Because directly after Christmas," said Winnie proudly, "he makes his first professional appearance."

Alistair had no need to whip up his enthusiasm. In that last pregnant sentence he read the glorious continuity of English history.

"I say, that's splendid!" he cried, resisting an impulse to shake her by the hand.

"It's not one of the big fights, o' course," explained Winnie. "Just one of the fill-ups against a boy called Hackney Jack. But Mr. Moss—he's the gentleman who saw Eddie fight at the Club and fixed it up—says that if he wins he can chuck the bookstall from then on. And Eddie'll wipe the floor with him." She stopped suddenly, and Alistair, following her glance, saw a tall thin figure hurrying down the road.

"Well, I guess I got to go," said Winnie. "Don't do anything your mother wouldn't like—"

"I say, that isn't Eddie," said Alistair, "that's Arnold Comstock."

"Oh, I'm not meeting Eddie *here*, I'm meeting him at the hall," explained Winnie hastily; and pulling her jacket to the fashionable tightness, pattered off on her jewelled heels.

Alistair waited a moment before going in, half-flattered by her having stayed so long to talk to him, and considerably amused by her evening or manikin deportment. Instead of her usual puppy-jumps, Winnie now moved in a series of rhythmic undulations, body leant well back from the hips and legs moving with measured elegance. It was a walk she had learnt out of *Beautiful Womanhood*, and practiced for five minutes every night of her life. Having now become more or less proficient, she would have welcomed more frequent opportunities for display: but an innate sense of humour limited her field. A really long frock, however, made all the difference, and as Alistair watched her slow down and halt for a few words with Mr. Comstock, he suddenly recaptured the modish apparition who had met him on the doorstep. At fifty yards the illusion was complete.

Vaguely disturbed by this fresh example of feminine camouflage, he let himself into the house, and climbed slowly upstairs. First Miss Tibbald, now Winnie. . . . It occurred to him rather forcibly that he ought to know a great deal more about women.

CHAPTER V

I

THE prospect of his introduction to literary life occupied Alistair's thoughts almost exclusively for the next few days. Henry, however, remained quite calm, expressing a proper gratitude but mentioning in almost the same breath that his Training College was about to give a performance of *The Devil's Disciple*. For some reason this very common occurrence seemed to fill him with excitement, though he himself was no more than a walker-on; and Alistair learnt with dismay that rehearsals would continue for a month.

On Friday morning, however, life was definitely brightened by the arrival of two handsome cards inviting them both to become temporary members of the Embryo Club. There were neat dotted lines for name and profession, proposer and seconder; and Alistair was interested to learn that they were being sponsored by E.C. Tibbald and Matthew Barclay. The latter name attracted him not a little, and he wondered whether by any chance he and Mr. Barclay were destined to rise to fame like David and Jonathan. . . . It would be hard on Henry, of course, but in this world a man has to find his own level. Alistair took the cards to the writing-table and began to fill them in.

Name: Henry Brough. Profession: Student.

Name: Alistair French. Profession: . . .

"I've put myself down as a playwright," he told Henry that evening. (It was seven o'clock, the meeting did not begin till eight-thirty, but he had already changed his collar.) "I don't know whether I mentioned it, but I've come to the conclusion that that's my real line."

It was quite true: almost immediately after their arrival in Bloom Street, Alistair had come to the conclusion that he would stop writing novels and write plays. Plays, as he now pointed out to his friend, admitted of a more direct attack on the emotions, satisfied eye and ear as well as intellect, and were altogether far more suitable vehicles for his art.

"They're much shorter to write, too," added Henry.

Alistair looked at him sharply. It was either the first or the last thing on earth one would expect from Henry, but he had no means of ascertaining which.

"Next Sunday," continued Henry, "I shall read the *Observer* in the morning and go for a short walk. After lunch I shall go to sleep; and in the evening I shall do three hours' theory."

That at least was quite in his old style, but Alistair, who was just about to clean a pair of shoes, reached for the communal Nugget in a slightly ruffled frame of mind. Even to himself he had not yet admitted that this difference in length—a difference of no less than forty thousand words—might be one of the decisive factors in his change of mind; but there was no doubt that he felt himself more at home in the shorter medium. And why not? Beside Dostoievsky, Maupaussant: beside Dante, Sappho; it was as absurd to judge a poem by its length as a statue by its weight.

"It's as absurd," he told Henry, "to judge a poem by its length as a statue by its weight. Lots of the biggest men have employed relatively minor forms, and I must say I find them at least as attractive."

"You ought to write parables," said Henry. He dusted his boots with a pyjama-jacket and added that since the show didn't start till eight-thirty there would be plenty of time to eat at the Riviera.

Rather sulkily (for there were several other things about himself which he wanted to say) Alistair put on his shoes and followed his friend downstairs. On so momentous an occasion, too, he would have preferred to dine somewhere a little more significant; but before he could decide to advance this theory they were halfway down the road, and another minute saw Henry bounding towards the Café door.

They had happened on the rush hour, and were consequently forced to share a table with Winnie and Charlie Coe, who had just finished but stayed on out of pure sociability. (At the next table there were actually three places vacant, but the fourth being occupied by Mr. Hickey made them diffident.) Winnie, who appeared to be in unusual spirits, at once turned her back on her original dinner-partner and began to tell them about a coat she had seen in Kimberly Street. It was of bright red cloth, with a deep collar of leopard skin and cuffs to match, and the shopwoman—Madame Louise, she was, about half-way down on the right-hand side—had offered to let her have it for ten-and-six a month.

"Yes, and how many months for?" asked Charlie Coe suspiciously.

"Eight," said Winnie over her shoulder. "O' course, if I paid right away I could get it for three-ten. It's quite a difference."

"What happens," asked Mr. Hickey from the next table, "if you die before you finish paying?"

They all looked round in flattered surprise. It was very seldom that he considered the conversation worth joining.

"I never thought to ask," said Winnie; "they'd come and take it back, most like. Anyway, I shouldn't care."

"I don't see they ought to do that," said Mr. Hickey, who liked to get his teeth into a subject. "You might have paid as much as six months of it You want to go into the thing properly, my girl."

Charlie nodded agreement.

"I don't hold with all this hire-purchase, anyway," he said. "If you want a thing, you save up your money and pay for it. Then it's yours, see? That's what I say."

"I've got two-pound-five in the Post Office," contributed Winnie, considerably pleased by the interest she had aroused.

"Then you leave it there," said Mr. Hickey; and retired from the conversation.

Alistair and Henry, meanwhile, had disposed of two tomato soups and were silently filling themselves with steak-and-kidney pie. They were both privately convinced that Winnie's coat must be one of the most appalling garments ever stitched together, and hoped by a protective self-effacement to avoid being asked their opinion. The ruse failed completely.

"What d'you think?" demanded Winnie, squirming round in her chair so that she could gaze directly into Alistair's face. "D'you think I'd look nice in red? It wouldn't come right up to my hair, o' course, because of the fur. That's ever so nice, all spotty."

"Leopard, isn't it?" he supplied intelligently.

"That's right. An' I thought a black hat, with perhaps a little red feather. *All* red would be too much."

"It would be a bit," agreed Alistair, taking a large mouthful of pie.

"An' black shoes. Coo! I wouldn't half look a dog. The only thing is, will it suit my hair? Because it's ever so fair, isn't it? And it must be getting lighter, too, because when I was a nipper it was that dark you wouldn't believe. Here, swallow that down and tell me if you think I'd look smart."

Alistair swallowed.

"I think you'd look extremely striking," he pronounced at last. "Especially with a black hat. They'd see you coming a mile off."

Winnie was extremely gratified.

"It's got real style," she said, "you'll see. But I won't get it on the installment, I'll save up like Charlie said."

"And then find it's sold, most like," prophesied Clara. She was the Riviera waitress, and had been following the conversation with much interest.

"No, it won't," cried Winnie. "The shopwoman's promised to keep it for me."

"Yes, and you wait till any one comes in with cash down," said Clara. "That's what happened to me over a blue velvet skirt not two months ago. What to follow, please?"

They both ordered cold apple tart.

"There you are," said Charlie, as soon as she had gone. "These installment places are no go. You go along with the money in your hand, and you know where you are. For all you know you may see another you like better."

"Not better than the red I shan't." Winnie shook her head decidedly. "Never as long as I live."

"I'd paid a deposit, too," continued Clara, returning with the portions of tart. "Would you believe it!"

Under cover of these revelations Henry and Alistair finished their meal undisturbed and began to think about moving. It was getting on for eight, and the Embryo Club met in Kensington.

"What, you finished already?" exclaimed Winnie in surprise. "We'll walk back with you."

As carelessly as possible, Alistair explained that they were not returning directly to Number Fifteen, and thus drew a natural inquiry as to their plans.

"Why, wherever are you off to?" asked Winnie.

"Tiger-shooting," replied Henry, with unexpected resource.

"Garn! You're having me on." She looked from one to the other, wriggling with curiosity, while Charlie frowned at her across the table. "I believe you're going to meet your girl friends!"

"Got it in one," said Alistair, assuming as conquering an air as he knew how.

"Come on, tell us her name!"

"Clara Bow," said Alistair, one hand on the door.

"No, but honest!"

"Greta Garbo."

"Oh, get back into the oven," said Winnie. "You're half-baked."

II

Apart from the enjoyment Alistair had had in filling them up, the cards seemed more or less pointless, for no one asked to look at them, and Miss Tibbald was waiting at the door. She met Alistair like an old friend, and expressed great pleasure in making Henry's acquaintance: after which they all three moved into the temporary clubroom (kindly lent by a teacher of Eurythmics), and sat down.

In a flutter of excitement Alistair pushed his chair back against the wall and looked about him.

There were nearly two hundred people in the room, for Henry Montague was a draw of the first class, but in spite of its considerable animation the *coup d'oeil* was not inspiring. Besides Henry and himself there were only two other young persons present, an Indian lad of about sixteen and a girl in a rather dashing hat. The rest of the company were aged between forty and seventy, and Alistair observed with a queer alarm that they all wore an air of gentle satisfaction. The older the member, indeed, the more contented its expression: a few in the early forties had a slightly restless look, as though they were still a little worried about themselves; but after forty-five some soothing influence appeared to get to work, and the furrowed brows were smoothed to complacency. There was one old lady who had even brought her needlework, and as he watched her calm, absorbed face Alistair suddenly discovered the reason of his alarm. They looked happy and contented, all these people, not because they had won through, but because they had given up.

"Interesting, isn't it?" said Miss Tibbald, who had been explaining to Henry about the aims of the Club. "Mr. Barclay ought to be here soon, and then I'll introduce you. I'm so afraid he'll be late, because they've got the auditors in, and Henry Montague is always so punctual—" Her voice died away in a little gasp of excitement, and she plucked Alistair eagerly by the sleeve, "Look, there he is now, just coming in with the Chairman. Look, Mr. Brough, that's Henry Montague!"

Not without excitement Alistair followed her gaze and saw a stockily built man of about fifty moving towards the lecturer's table. He had a good head, thick grey eyebrows, and a mouth that shut fast in one long, slightly humorous line. The tide of disillusion was checked, and Alistair drew a long breath.

"How well his dinner-jacket fits!" murmured Miss Tibbald.

She was quite right, the garment sat superbly on Mr. Montague's square shoulders. Though far from being a dandy, he was known as one of the best-dressed figures in literature, and as the Chairman said a few conventional words the Club noted with approval a remarkably fine gardenia. It was all up to specification.

Amid a really creditable volume of applause, therefore, the great novelist, who happened to be very shortsighted, put on a pair of tortoiseshell spectacles and unfolded his speech.

"Ladies and gentlemen," he said, "to the young most things are irrelevant, and I shall not trouble you with the supreme irrelevance of an opening remark. But to the young all things are also possible, and I therefore propose to give you some useful advice on how to behave when you are all famous."

He looked up, and for the first time saw his audience through glasses. The audience was smiling pleasantly back, obviously amused by his prologue, and eager for him to continue. With an explanatory cough Henry Montague reached for the carafe, and poured himself out a glass of water. He tried hard to remember what his secretary had told him he was going to say, but with no result. All about youth, no doubt, youth and success and adventures to the venturous . . . all utterly impossible. But on the other hand it was equally impossible for him to speak extempore . . . he could never pull it off, even at Oxford. . . .

The last drops of water were trickling down his throat as he saw his way out. With a sigh of relief the great man removed his glasses, and holding the typescript a little nearer, resumed his interrupted speech.

As soon as the final applause had died away the meeting relaxed and turned into a social gathering. Large trays of coffee and cake were brought in, and after a hopeful interval Alistair discovered that these were for sale. It seemed only polite, considering all her kindness, to treat Miss Tibbald to a piece of Swiss roll, and with a word of explanation he made his way towards the improvised buffet. There were a number of people already ordering, and as he waited to be served he amused himself by thinking which members he would shoot if given unlimited powers for the suppression of undesirables. The two front rows fell in swathes, in the third he spared only an elderly poet and the Indian youth. The fourth went entirely, and the fifth; but in the sixth he was suddenly pulled up by a face which he could not only tolerate but actually liked. It was squarish, very tanned, with mutton-chop whiskers, and it belonged to a man of forty or so in a brown overcoat. Alistair looked at him, and he looked back at Alistair, and it was at once plain that he knew all about the shooting. Rather shamefacedly Alistair threw away his gun and bought three cups of coffee (Henry, he trusted, would refund the twopence later) and a piece of chocolate cake.

When he got back to their table, however, he found Miss Tibbald was already nibbling a macaroon, and his place taken by a wistful little gentleman in grey. Henry, with his usual lack of *savoir-faire*, had found an old evening paper and was doing the crossword.

"Oh, you *poor* boy!" cried Miss Tibbald. "*How* they've kept you waiting! And now Mr. Barclay sitting on your chair!"

She introduced them with some pride, playwright and man of letters, while Alistair distributed his burden. (He put the cake in front of Henry, hoping that he would eat it automatically and then have to pay. It was not meanness, but one of the results of living on a hundred a year.)

"What did you think of the speaker?" asked the man of letters.

Alistair hesitated with unnecessary delicacy; and said finally that it had been very interesting.

"Oh, the address," said Mr. Barclay. "Very interesting indeed. But I was speaking for the moment of the man himself. One can't help feeling sorry for him."

Alistair goggled. Sorry for the great Henry Montague? *Sorry* for him? In Heaven's name, why?

"An outsider, for instance," proceeded Mr. Barclay, "might even think of him as genuinely successful."

Considering the perfect dinner-jacket, remembering all he had heard about the Montague royalties, Alistair agreed that an outsider might very well be deceived in that way.

"Whereas we who know—we of the same trade—recognize that he's done absolutely nothing. All these plays that run a year apiece—what are they? A string of moderately bright remarks spoken by expensively gowned young women with good figures." He cleared his throat. "Nothing he's done will be read a year after he's dead, and the poor devil knows it. Because, mark you," said Mr. Barclay handsomely, "the man isn't altogether a fool."

"It must worry him dreadfully," said kind Miss Tibbald.

Over the rim of his coffee-cup Alistair watched her steal an admiring glance at the iconoclast. Mr. Barclay was staring straight ahead in a stern, incorruptible kind of way, and the dramatic lighting of a table-lamp strengthened his small beaky face with abrupt shadows. He looked for all the world like a hanging judge.

But Alistair doubted.

He did not want to doubt, he wanted to worship. No neophyte had ever approached the shrine with purer motives. He wanted to sit at the feet of great men and drink in their wisdom. But there was something about the Embryo Club that roused his suspicions. The great age of most of its members, for instance, the placid contentment of the lady with the needlework. Here was neither the dust nor the glory, but a middle state of undistinguished security. They all looked as though they had just enough to live on.

A growing malaise invaded his soul. He wanted to be gone, at once, before he lost all courage. It was nearly ten, there would be no discourtesy.... With sudden decision he glanced at Miss Tibbald, and finding her deep in conversation with the poet, kicked Henry under the table.

Henry looked up in some surprise, and Alistair stared meaningly at the clock. Henry shook his head, and tilted the paper to show his crossword half completed. He wanted to stay and finish it.

"Bring it with you," mouthed Alistair silently; and rising to his feet told Miss Tibbald they were most frightfully sorry, but they had to get back.

III

In the days that followed neither Alistair nor Henry ever made any reference to this excursion: a silence which, while only natural in Alistair, was in Henry yet another proof of an exceptionally nice nature. About a week later they received a friendly letter from the secretary of the club, enclosing a book of by-laws and two application forms, to which Alistair replied with an equally friendly postcard saying that both himself and Mr. Brough were unfortunately leaving Town almost at once. He also avoided, with complete success, that part of the Gardens where he had met Miss Tibbald, which might have been ingratitude but was also human nature.

Henry meanwhile was becoming more and more wrapped up in the life of the Training College, where he had made many interesting friends. They were all rather prominent people, genuine Bloomsburyites as opposed to the brown-baggers who went home every day on the five-twenty-three. Most of them seemed to live round Torrington Square, in which congenial atmosphere they had built up a queer, acutely self-conscious student life of their own, neatly grafted on to a sound middle-class upbringing and centering round one or two cheap Italian restaurants.

With these bold spirits Alistair too was soon on familiar terms, accompanying Henry to their evening parties and attending such college functions as were open to the general public. He learned to talk irreverently of the Senate, and also what was meant by the initials N.U.S., U.C., K.C.W., W.U.S.S., U.L.U., S.C.M., and many others. Once he went to a conversazione disguised as a Theolog. In his heart of hearts, however, he remained an outsider, and as an outsider it pleased him to find them all a trifle parochial, a trifle over-absorbed in college politics and their own minor verse. But he envied them all the same.

He envied them because, however they might appear to the detached observer, they did really and truly feel that they were leading a genuine *vie de bohème*, and therefore enjoyed themselves as much as any one out of Murger. To defend the League of Nations over six-pennyworth of spaghetti left both body and soul in a state of grand complacency, while the reading of Villon in a gallery queue exalted the spirits like new wine. They also had the sort of love affairs in which each party continued to pay for his or her own meals, and often became engaged in their third term. In short, they were for the most part extremely happy, and Alistair had just received his first disillusionment.

It was about this time that he put aside his novel (it was about a young man who set out to seek his fortune) and began work on a comedy of manners about a young man who left home and became a Dictator of the Press. He sometimes wondered whether it could possibly be produced by early spring, but decided this would be asking too much even of hurrying Fame. In any case, the following autumn would be well within the year allowed him by Uncle Severus.

CHAPTER VI

I

THERE were in London at this time countless trios of young women living together in top-floor flats and addressing one another as Pooh, Eeyore, and Christopher Robin. Many of them earned their own living, others painted book-ends, or attended courses at the University; but the ones Henry knew (as was only natural) were all going to teach. He seemed rather pleased with the acquaintance.

"They give parties every other Saturday," he told Alistair. "I'm going tomorrow. Would you like to come along?"

"God forbid!" said Alistair; but more because it sounded well than because he meant it.

"They're rather friends of mine," said Henry stiffly, "and extremely intelligent. Most people find their parties rather amusing." He was too generous to rake up the past, but the evening at the Embryo was fresh in both their minds.

"I'm sure it'll be marvellous," agreed Alistair repentantly. "What exactly happens?"

"They read plays—awfully advanced stuff, I believe. Tomorrow it's the *Country Wife*."

"Isn't that Restoration?" asked Alistair, beginning to wish he had been rather less absolute.

"Oh, frightfully. But you can get it in the Everyman edition for two bob." Henry paused, his natural benevolence once more getting the upper hand. "Look here, I know what I'll do. I'll tell them you're working frightfully hard, but you'll come if you can manage it. Then they won't have to keep a part or anything." Alistair looked a bit bored.

"Do, if it's not too much trouble," he said. "Though you'll probably be right about the work. I've just got an idea for another play."

But of course he went all the same.

II

Contrary to his expectations, he was much impressed by the size and luxury of the Pooh flat. The room in which the reading was to take place was a large square apartment papered in biscuit colour, and bright with chrysanthemums. It was furnished in two distinct styles, the more important pieces being of mahogany, the lighter and less expensive of weathered oak. Round the walls hung several etchings and rhyme-sheets, together with neatly executed memoranda to the effect that This is Pooh's Week for Breakfast and that Eeyore Must Not Use the Bath After Eleven. The general effect was thus one of great camaraderie, and when Alistair and Henry arrived many of the guests were already sitting on the floor.

They were, indeed, the last to come, and Henry was greeted with a volley of cheerful abuse from all three hostesses.

"Pooh and Eeyore have been cursing you steadily for the last half-hour," cried Christopher Robin.

"The people next door began to knock on the wall in horror," added Pooh, a pleasant-faced young woman obviously formed by nature for the instruction of kindergartens.

"Really," finished up Eeyore, evidently feeling the onus of her reputation, "really, Henry, you're the biggest b.f. in the whole b. college. We tell you specially to come early, and you calmly turn up at a quarter-past!" She turned to Alistair with a reassuring smile. "I don't know how you put up with him, Mr. French. Isn't he a mess?"

"Oh, I survive," said Alistair; but before he could go on and be funny too he found himself seized and silenced by Christopher Robin. (Or it might have been Pooh. They all looked very much alike.)

"Come and be introduced," said one or other of them kindly. "This is Mary Long, Jimmy Horner, Bubbles, Fenton, Cressida Drury, your old friend Henry . . ." She led him rapidly round the group at the fire, pausing with each name, and then moving on before he had time to look at the owner. However, he grinned nervously, accepted a cigarette, and finally sat down beside the youth Fenton.

"Are you up at London?" asked Mr. Fenton.

"No," said Alistair, hoping to be asked the obvious question; in which case he intended to say firmly: "I write." But instead Mr. Fenton waited for him to speak, and Alistair was cornered.

"Classics," replied Mr. Fenton gloomily. "Theoretically, that is, and whenever I have a spare moment." The major part of his time, it appeared, was devoted to the editing of a college paper. This was an extremely difficult thing to do, partly on account of the fatheadedness of the students and partly because of his own unconventionality. He also told Alistair how difficult it was to express oneself in words.

"My God, yes!" said Alistair; but without result.

"The only writer of genius we've had since Sterne," continued Mr. Fenton, "is D.H. Lawrence. I sent a wreath to his funeral."

"You knew him, then?" cried Alistair, surprised into envy. But Mr. Fenton frowned.

"Not personally. He didn't live in England at the last." There was a slight pause, a chill had evidently fallen on the conversation, and after a few minutes the follower of Lawrence rose in search of matches, and did not return.

Alistair was not sorry to be left alone. It was time his analytical eye got to work. The dozen or so people in the room were all, individually, types with which he was not unfamiliar. Most of them probably came from homes very like his own; not one would have seemed out of place at Aunt Gertrude's tea-table; and yet there was something— an air, an atmosphere—about the gathering as a whole that made him feel a stranger. The word Bohemian rose in his mind, only to be rejected; there was a liberality, a breadth of culture in their talk, but certainly no license. Many of their allusions—to Unions, Presidents, Dramatics, and the Debating—were naturally out of his reach, and he knew his loneliness to be merely that of a small boy from a different prep. school; but from these very allusions, no less than from the references to Proust and living in sin, sprang something so disproportionately impressive that Alistair was in danger of being completely overwhelmed by it; and very likely would have been, had he not happened to notice, just at this moment, that two of the etchings on the biscuit-coloured walls represented the same subject—i.e. Peter Pan in Kensington Gardens. The incident, trivial though it was, somehow restored his confidence.

"Ah, but you ought to meet my Ma Parker," cried Henry from the other side of the room.

That was another odd experience, to see old Henry moving easily and naturally on these new levels. Without actually flitting, he moved happily from group to group, always ready with appropriate greeting or apt retort; and Alistair was astounded to hear, as he progressed, familiar inquiries after Winnie and Charlie Coe.

He himself, of course, had always realized their conversational value, but that Henry should have done so too struck him as curiously unexpected. It was also slightly annoying, and Alistair returned to his analysis with a new detachment.

"Rather nondescript," he decided, letting his eye stray coolly over the group by the fire. Two of the men had side-whiskers, and one wore in addition a black jersey with a high neck; but it looked more like the gift of a careful mother than anything to do with the Fascisti. As for the women, they were all (a phenomenon already marked in Pooh, Eeyore, and Christopher Robin) curiously alike, with short hair, fresh complexions, and a tendency to wear brown and orange. . . .

And then he saw Cressida.

She was standing at the other end of the semi-circle, apparently having just left her seat to move farther from the fire; and the first thing that struck him about her was an air of natural elegance that made all the other women look amorphous, ill-groomed, and too brightly coloured. A closer inspection showed her to be wearing a dress of some plain black material, fitted to her slenderness like a black glove, and frilled from elbow to wrist with bands of creamy net that fell about her hands like the ruffles of an eighteenth-century fop. Alistair's heart turned slowly over.

"Has any one read the text?" asked Eeyore briskly, so soon as all the guests had been chivvied into their seats. The murmur of conversation died away in muted apology, and when the silence was complete Miss Drury said quietly:

"Yes, I have."

Eeyore looked round reproachfully.

"No one else? Well, I can't talk, because I haven't myself, but I'm afraid we shall have to take parts rather at random."

At random they did so. Miss Drury was Lady Fidget, Henry (to Alistair's fury) Sir Jasper Fidget, and Alistair himself Mr. Dorilant. The young man in the black sweater then observed that as his name actually was Horner, he might as well read Horner; and the rest of the parts were distributed in strict rotation, leaving Christopher Robin with the composite role of Boy, Quack, Lucy, Waiters, and Attendants.

"Good," said Eeyore. "All got the place? Enter Horner, Quack following from a distance. Come on, Horner!"

Mr. Horner coughed and extinguished his cigarette.

"A quack is as fit for a pimp," he read, *"as a midwife for a bawd; they are still but in their way, both helpers of nature. Well, my dear Doctor, hast thou done as I desired?"*

"I have undone you for ever with the women, and reported you throughout the whole town as bad as an eunuch," replied Christopher Robin bravely, *"with as much trouble as if I had made you one in earnest."*

III

As the reading progressed, an odd stillness settled over the company. Students and free-thinkers all, they tackled the text with exemplary coolness: but at the back of each mind lay the unspoken thought that it was far worse than they had expected. One curious phenomenon was that through a fear of appearing prudish or embarrassed, all readers were liable, when coming to any specially period expression, to pronounce it more loudly than the rest of the sentence; in one or two cases, moreover, the young ladies were quite rightly unsure of their pronunciation—the initial *w*, for instance, was it sounded or silent?—and showed a marked tendency to underline by pause.

But to every poison an antidote, and it was soon discovered that by employing a very low, matter-of-fact delivery one could do much to neutralize Restoration and even Biblical phraseology. Led by Mr. Horner, the whole company began to read as from a very dull Baedeker, and with the help of this polite fiction might have got along very well had it not been for the girl in the black dress. As soon as she opened her lips it became apparent that the guide-book style made little appeal: she read, on the contrary, with so much spirit and understanding as to make things very difficult for the other protagonists. When Eeyore, for instance, called Mr. Horner a rude beast, it sounded like Fourth Form slang: but when Miss Drury addressed him (only two lines farther on) as a rotten French wether, it somehow transposed the whole passage into quite a different key. Her diction, moreover, being remarkably good, it was almost impossible not to hear every word she said, so that in Lady Fidget's speeches many of the grosser adjectives were made public for the first time.

The stillness deepened: but Alistair at least was lost to all decent feelings. At the first sound of that exquisite voice his heart had missed its beat, and even at the end of Act Three was behaving with marked irregularity. At every movement of those long narrow hands—whether to turn the page or point an indecent jest—a strange feeling of emptiness supervened immediately below his ribs. He thought her (and in this, oddly enough, he was quite correct) the most beautiful thing he had ever seen: the most adorable, talented, and morally perfect of all earth's creatures: the nonpareil, in short, of creation; and therefore had no choice but to fall head over heels in love.

"Mr. Dorilant!" called Pooh sharply.

"Engaged to women, and not sup with us!" read Alistair thankful it was no worse. Glancing down the page, however, he saw that Baedeker would soon be his only hope, and for the next few minutes was obliged to concentrate entirely on the difficulties of the text.

They were very great, particularly in those scenes which took place in Horner's apartment; but the little band plowed bravely on and droned its way gallantly through every variety of improper situation. At the beginning of Scene Four, Act Five, however, Christopher Robin, who had evidently been looking ahead, put down her book and raised a cry of coffee.

It was taken up with alacrity, but specially by Mr. Horner: plates of chocolate biscuits appeared as though by magic, and in the enjoyment of these delicacies all cares were soon forgotten. Mr. Wycherley ceased to trouble, Mr. Horner, in his proper person, obliged with a brilliant imitation of a well-known professor. A girl who had spent the summer in Normandy told them all about the French peasants there. Henry and Eeyore tried to sing the Volga Boat Song; and Alistair talked to Cressida Drury.

He had opened the conversation quite naturally by offering her a cup of coffee, and was now actually seated beside her on the sofa: for there was not that press of admirers which might have been expected. The other men were indeed constantly glancing in their direction, but not one of them, thought Alistair conceitedly, had sufficient courage to leave the new-gained haven of college chatter. . . .

Unlike Mr. Fenton, she at once asked what he did.

"I write plays," said Alistair.

"Tell me," said Miss Drury, her beautiful eyes widening ever so slightly. They were of a clear grey colour, the edge of the iris so distinct that it appeared to be rimmed with a fine black line, and set wide apart under brows of extreme whiteness.

Miss Drury repeated her request.

Flushing brilliantly, Alistair put down his cup, and embarked on a very long and complicated sentence, from which the fact emerged that he had not as yet had anything actually produced.

"Of *course* not," she said understanding. (Her hair was black and glossy as a bird's wing.) "No one has anything produced until they're sixty-five and waiting for burial." But her eyes challenged him all the same, and he knew in that instant he would succeed before thirty or die in the attempt. With simple conceit he said, therefore:

"Of course, I know it's quite impossible."

"I adore the impossible," answered Miss Drury calmly.

He then began to talk with some brilliance and no sense of time, for she was a listener to make eloquent the Sphinx; and had just warmed up to the stage of continuous epigram when Henry came up with the observation that every one had gone home.

IV

About half-way down the stairs Alistair began to be considerably annoyed by the presence of his friend. Miss Drury was already nearly a flight ahead, and there seemed no conventionally valid reason why he should leave the one to hasten after the other. The predicament was undoubtedly full of symbolism, and at a lower pitch of feeling he could have analyzed it with the best; but with an actual Cressida vanishing before his eyes there was no room for anything but mortal pain, and he was just about to expire from pure emotion when far above their heads a voice, called over the banisters.

"Henry!"

Henry stopped.

"You've left one of your gloves!"

Seizing his opportunity, Alistair bounded ahead, and reached the front door with two seconds to spare. Cressida had paused to draw on a white glove, and now turned calmly, all unaware of the surrounding tempest, with the remark that it was a fine night.

"Marvellous," agreed Alistair; and panted loudly.

"I was afraid it might still be raining."

"Were you?" said Alistair.

They then proceeded in silence to the end of the road. There was a pillar-box at the corner, and here Cressida fortunately stopped to post a letter, thus giving him time to take his bearings. If he were going straight home he ought to turn to the right and make for Warren Street: if— if anything else. . . .

The letter dropped inside the box with a small decisive plop.

"Have you far to go?" asked Alistair.

"Only ten minutes' walk. I live in Carey Street."

He swallowed fiercely.

"May I see you home?"

"That would be very nice of you," said Cressida.

At first they continued to exchange desultory sentences about London and its 'bus routes, but the echoing squares did not encourage them, and after a few minutes they walked in companionable silence. The empty pavements rang underfoot, and presently Alistair noticed that they had fallen into a slow rhythm, a slow, buoyant stride that carried them along like two ships riding the same tide. It was the motion of a dream, but of a dream in which the most trivial details were vivid and remarkable. Under one of the lamp-posts lay a fallen plane leaf, in colour the exact tone of a worn leather binding; the rain, drying off the rest of the pavement, had outlined it with a narrow border of wet; and this now appeared to him in its true light as an object of exquisite beauty. A little farther on a second lamp, this time jutting from a corner pharmacy, cast a long peculiar shadow; he saw at once that it was the shadow of an old Grenadier, shako on head, and pack on shoulder. He did not mention these things to Cressida, there was no need.

When they came to her door she turned and said: "Won't you come up and smoke a cigarette?"

Alistair followed her in.

CHAPTER VII

I

As THEY climbed the three twisting flights of stairs every fiber and nerve in his body was separately conscious of the lateness of the hour. It was, in fact, nearly midnight; but when they finally reached the top floor Cressida ushered him into her room with a sang-froid so great that she was not herself aware of it.

"Wait by the door, please," she ordered, "while I light the gas. It's the curse of my life."

"We have it too," said Alistair. "One's always losing the matches."

There was a loud pop, and she reappeared in a bright yellow glow.

"Now come in and sit on the divan while I get you a drink. Tell me about your writing."

He obeyed, seating himself with extreme care, for he had a pretty good idea that the black-draped structure under the window was also her bed. The whole contrast, indeed, between Miss Drury and her chamber was so extraordinary that for a moment he could think of nothing else. Without actually considering the matter, but judging unconsciously from her appearance, he had pictured long dressing-tables gleaming with silver, mirrors from floor to ceiling, cupboards lined with cedar-wood; and here was the merest painted bamboo of a top-floor bedroom. Instead of the great wardrobe, one corner was cut off by a faded blue curtain: and under Alistair's weight the divan gave forth the unmistakable clanking groan of an iron bedstead.

"I hope you like gin," said Cressida.

She moved across the shabby room like a figure from another world, carrying two little glasses of colourless liquid and still wearing her black coat. He eyed it narrowly, and was confirmed in his original opinion that it was a very beautiful garment.

"All the best."

"All the best," repeated Alistair. He tossed off a mouthful of gin, and was relieved to find the taste agreeable. "Won't you sit down yourself?"

"In a minute," said Cressida. For that space of time she moved beautifully about the room, drawing the curtains, unearthing a box of cigarettes; then took off her coat and drew back the blue curtain, so that he could not help seeing behind it. There were exactly two dresses, one black, one long shimmering white thing all pinned round with tissue paper.

"What did you think of the reading?" she asked, fitting the shoulders of her coat to its hanger.

Alistair considered. He had, after all, partaken of their biscuits and coffee.

"I don't think," he said at last, "that it was quite the right sort of play for—for that sort of occasion—"

"I should think not." The wonderful voice was alive with disdainful amusement. "Poor things, they didn't know what they were in for. That Restoration stuff is the most difficult thing in the world. But it was funny in its way." She disposed of her coat and came back to the divan, sitting easily with her back against the wall and her long slim legs drawn up on to the cushions. By moving his hand about half an inch Alistair could just touch the heel of her left shoe. He did so. "Now tell me about your plays."

"But what about you?" he said. "You haven't told me anything yet"

She looked at him, curiously, out of her beautiful grey eyes.

"You're the first man I've ever known refuse an opportunity to talk about himself. I shall have to cultivate your acquaintance."

"You see what I gain by it," he pointed out.

Cressida laughed.

"You're very shy, aren't you? How did you come to be there tonight?"

Very briefly Alistair told her, sketching a swift, slightly ironic portrait of Henry, and an even slighter though more flattering one of himself; but he was really far more anxious to hear the explanation of her presence there than to account for his own. "You can't think how strange you looked," he told her boldly. "Like—like—" but the only comparison that came to his mind was the old one of the swan among geese; and though she did indeed resemble, in the most striking manner, a beautiful black swan, he felt the image to be too hackneyed for her approval.

"I used to know Pooh when I was at Bristol," said Cressida, calmly removing him from the predicament. "Her home's there you know, and I used to be in the Repertory. I hadn't seen her for two years till yesterday morning we ran into each other crossing the Strand, and in the excitement of the moment she invited me for tonight. An impulse," added Cressida thoughtfully, "which I am afraid has been since regretted."

"I thought you weren't an amateur," said Alistair.

"Amateur!" He had never heard such biting, histrionic scorn as quivered in the three syllables. "God, no! I've been on the stage three years, besides the Rep. But I'd go anywhere to read a part, even with—with a crowd like tonight's. It's all practice."

He hesitated, fearful of offending against professional etiquette, but at last ventured to ask whether she were actually in anything at the time.

"Of course not, my dear. If I were I couldn't have been there tonight." She sighed. "No, at the moment I'm resting."

In this last phrase Alistair detected a certain irony. Quite possibly she didn't want to rest at all.

"It must be awfully difficult," he risked, "to get a part in the West End."

"Difficult! It makes the eye of a needle look like the Admiralty Arch. Young women who think they can act without any training . . ." She shrugged one shoulder, a characteristic elegant-weary gesture. "They make me furious."

He knew not how to comfort her. It seemed to him intolerable that any one so lovely should be troubled by material cares; and yet already he was beginning to suspect that not for her was the lotus-heaven of quiescence. She needed the dust and clamor before victory.

"You shouldn't ask me questions that make me angry," said Cressida, smiling at him with her eyes. She reached for the cigarette-box, though they were both smoking, and bade him admire it.

"Ripping," said Alistair, taking the thing in his hand. It was made of some smooth dark wood, and rather beautifully proportioned.

"Some one brought it me from China. Have you been abroad much?"

"Very little," said Alistair. "I've been to Paris, of course." He had, in fact, helped take sixteen little boys on a week's visit in the previous spring, a trip which enabled them to combine instruction and pleasure at a remarkably low cost.

"Then let's talk about Paris. I adore it so, it always puts me in a good temper," said Cressida.

But this was not so easy as it sounded, for Alistair was very soon made aware that the Paris adored by his hostess and the Paris covered by his young charges were by no means the same city. Their list of historic monuments, for instance, did not include Mistinguett, nor had they ever dined elsewhere than at the *pension de famille* selected by Messrs. Cook; so he presently dropped his end of the conversation altogether and gave himself up to the pleasures of hearing.

The great charm of her voice, he decided, was its extraordinary variety of tone. It was not rich, it was not golden; in the reading of anything completely unemotional—the multiplication table, for instance—he could imagine it quite clear and colourless: but as she now talked, and earlier in the evening as Lady Fidget, her range of inflection was so great that one had the impression of listening to music. She spoke of the little cafés on Montparnasse, and the words tanged *pizzicato* on a muted string: in ceremonious violin phrases she described the great dressmakers' where she had never yet bought a frock; and then violin sweetened to harp, and his heart melted like snow, as she told him how exquisite was spring in the Palais-Royal,

"Every April," she said, "I have to fight against an impulse to rush over to Paris and take a flat in one of the attics. It would be so wonderful to wake up every morning feeling like a courtier of Louis Quinze . . . and then to look out of the window and see those thin rows of trees, just beginning to show green, and the fountain in the middle. One would have to be on the sunny side, of course."

"Of course," agreed Alistair seriously.

"I'm told there's no washing accommodation whatever, but perhaps if one got up early enough it might be possible to bathe in the fountain." Cressida laughed softly, stretching all her body in one swift luxurious movement. "I should like that. . . ."

"I shall know where to look for you next April," said he.

"Ah, no, you won't." Already, between one inflection and the next, her mood had darkened again; and already her whole attitude reflected the new humour. She leant forward, chin on fist, brooding angrily under her down-drawn brows. "Next April I shall be just where I am now, hanging round the agents and reading other women's names in electric lights. Women who act just about as well as I used to act at the Convent."

"When they put up the lights for *you*," began Alistair.

Quickly she turned on him.

"Yes, when? That's what I want to know. When?"

"Within the next two years." The prophecy, as it happened, was perfectly correct, but since Cressida could not know this it brought scant comfort. What she did know, on the other hand, was that young men in love made very poor critics.

"You don't understand," she said coldly. "It's not—it's not like that at all. Success . . ." And still turning to face him, she began to talk with a fierce strange earnestness that he had never before encountered, a fury of emotion beside which his own vague stirrings, though they had driven him all the way from Norbury, paled to the merest idle dreaming. She said that if she did not succeed before she was twenty-six she would die of chagrin, and he believed her utterly. She said she did not care what she paid, she would never haggle about the price, so long as she attained her end; and again he believed. He did not consider it likely, however, that the matter would ever be put to the test, for she was so beautiful that a manager had only to look at her to see his fortune. But when Alistair tried to explain this to her (very timidly and with some fears of being too personal), she merely smiled and fell silent.

"But I'll see you a star all the same," he insisted.

"Yes. I shall be a star all the same." A sudden melancholy seemed to come over her, and she sat a moment or two in silence. Alistair would very much have liked to pat her shoulder or show some other mark of sympathy, but was afraid of offending. It would be dreadful, in a young girl's room, and at that hour of the night, to appear to take the slightest liberty.

Cressida sighed and came out of her dream.

"I wonder what plays I shall star in?"

"Mine," said Alistair.

In that instant his shyness left him, and he began telling her of all the parts he would write for her in the years of their collaboration. She should portray every emotion under the sun, run the whole gamut from tragedy to comedy of manners, enriching all with her own particular touch, her own . . .

"My God, what is it?" cried Alistair. "Not formality, not manner—something you've got and all those other women hadn't. Something that's in everything you do or say, in the way you move your hands, the way you read tonight." He broke off, running his fingers recklessly through his hair, hunting his quarry down tracks too faint for words. Not beauty, not grace even, but something much more sophisticated. He paused a moment at sophistication itself, but that, though nearer the mark, was too narrow a term. Nor would breeding quite fit, nor elegance—and then suddenly he had it.

"Style," he said aloud. "That's what I was trying to think of. You must never play a part that hasn't style. You must never play, for instance, in anything of Barrie's."

Cressida had listened entranced, and did not now speak lest she should break the thread of his thought. But he had done for the time, and turned, overcome with fatigue, for the refreshment of her eyes.

"How lovely you are," he said simply.

And indeed, her face, so near that he could see the individual lashes, was too beautiful for him to contemplate any longer. Another minute, he felt, and he would be doing something unforgivable. His mind had already been crossed by the idea—not the intention or design, but the pure Platonic idea—of kissing her. With an heroic effort Alistair pulled himself together.

"It must be time I went," he said.

"Oh, time!" She dismissed eternity with a movement of the shoulder.

But he dared not. He thought of her reputation.

"Really I mustn't. I shall probably have to walk all the way home in any case."

She pressed him no more, but stretched luxuriously and stood up beside him. Her head came just to the level of his chin. Then he found his hat and followed her back down the twisting stairs.

"Good night, Cressida."

For an instant they stood so close in the darkness that he could hear the faint rhythm of her drawn breath.

"Good night, my dear."

She opened the door, and a gust of autumn-smelling air invaded the warm house. Alistair let go her hand and ran down the steps.

All the way back to Bloom Street, except when being directed by policemen, he sang extracts from the Scottish

Students' Song-book. Two melodies in particular caught his fancy—"Drink to me only," and "Passing by"—on which he concentrated for the last miles. Thus beguiled the way did not seem unduly long, but when at last he turned out the gas on the landing St. Peter's clock was chiming for the hour. It was two in the morning.

Very quietly Alistair opened the door. The room was in complete darkness, on the farther bed he could just distinguish the bumpy outline of his sleeping friend. It seemed a pity to wake him. Alistair closed the door softly and began to undress in the dark.

CHAPTER VIII

I

SUCH is the fallibility of human nature that every now and then a Sunday morning would dawn—as one did about five hours later—and find the Parker *ménage* clean out of bread; on which occasions it was Winnie's desperate practice to nip round to an accommodating little baker's and buy a couple of loaves under the counter. There was a whole ritual to be gone through—first a rapping on the closed shutters, then admittance through the little iron door, finally an anxious period of waiting in the darkened shop while the baker saw what he could spare. Winnie enjoyed every moment, and always adopted a special conspiratorial air that at once proclaimed her destination. Even Arnold Comstock noticed it as he lounged across the hall to get his milk.

"Run out of bread?" he asked, almost politely.

Winnie stopped, her hand on the latch.

"You said it. Ma and Mrs. Griffin they went an' made Welsh rabbits while I was at the pictures last night, and now there isn't scarcely a crumb. What they did with it I can't think, 'cept that Mrs. Griffin's got a nappetite like a nelephant. It was all our bread they used, too." She paused, swinging the basket nonchalantly against her shins. "Why don't you come and get a breath of air, Arnold? It's only just round the corner."

Arnold considered so long that her heart almost stopped beating. Then he ground the stub of his cigarette against the door-post and considered again.

"What time is it?" he asked. "I've got a meeting at eleven."

"Not more'n just after ten, Arnold. You'll be back long before."

The information appeared to decide him; and remarking that he had nothing better to do, Mr. Comstock accompanied her down Bloom Street.

II

It was very quiet behind the closed shutters, and so dark that a crack of yellow showed under the inner doorway. A warm and probably illegal odour of new bread enriched the air. The palms of Winnie's hands, pressing against the counter, took a grave pleasure in the smooth, man-serving wood. Continual scrubbing had worn long shallow grooves between the tougher ridges of the grain, and along these her fingers moved with a deep satisfaction. That was funny. The front of the counter was strengthened with a band of brass, also highly polished, but faintly greasy: and from its encounter Winnie's fingers started back in distaste. That was funny. It was perhaps the first time she had ever had leisure to analyze a physical reaction, for in her admirably ordered existence every cause and effect, event and reaction, was immediately followed by a second event and reaction, then a third, a fourth, and so on until bed-time. Had this incident of the counter occurred (as it very well might have) at the Riviera Café, it would have been quickly obliterated by the entrance of Charlie Coe, a pronouncement of Mr. Hickey's, or some other new emotion arising from her surroundings: but here, in the quiet and darkness, these instinctive sympathies and antipathies of her own hands took on a strange importance.

Her finger returned down one of the shallow lanes to an upstanding knot which it already knew of. Hard, yet polished, the knot thrust back into the ball: and at that the hand and arm, the whole impersonal body, was pleased. The hand moved on towards the brass border: at its first contact, just as before, the fingers leapt back, and the lips parted in a movement of disgust. All without her, Winnie, doing anything about it. As though her body didn't really belong to her at all.

As a counter-demonstration she at once drew in her hands and folded them tightly together. They wanted to go back to the wood, but she refused. The idea of her body as something quite separate seemed to her a great conception, worthy of people who wrote in the papers: and with an abrupt leap over the intervening processes she suddenly wondered whether that was why sometimes, at the last moment, when she had quite decided to let a fellow kiss her, she would push him off and dodge away. Because her lips weren't having any. And why she never let any one mess her about, not even Charlie, who really was keen on her and wanted to marry her. It was like her hand falling back from the greasy metal. Back to the clean wood. She didn't want Charlie because she wanted some one else.

Winnie raised her head and looked across at Arnold. He was leaning against the shutters in an attitude of profound melancholy, and his whole figure seemed to her infinitely noble and distinguished. It was a shame of the others to set on him as they did, especially Charlie and the boys. Mr. Hickey, of course, was old enough to be his father. . . .

The comparison pulled her up short. Mr. Hickey, for all his fine position and crotchety ways, couldn't be a day more than forty. Arnold—she remembered him saying so one night when they were arguing about Conchies—missed the War by eleven months. And the War had ended when she was just a kid, and they went on top of a 'bus to see the sights. Arnold must be getting on for thirty.

For the first time she saw him no longer as a boy, but as a man grown; a boy only in his freedom from responsibilities, his lack of consideration, his low earning powers. . . . "It's my belief he'd be better off on the dole," that's what Charlie used to say.

"And why?" countered Winnie hotly. "Because he's given up his life to others, that's why. All these Societies . . ."

The injustice of it amazed her. There was young Charlie Coe getting good money, and prospects in his garage, and no more ideals than a stuck pig. He helped at home, of course; but there was nothing noble about that, it was what every one did. There was Mr. Hickey, whom all looked up to so. There was Eddie Cribb, and the boys on the top floor. And now look at Arnold. Of the nature of his aims she knew very little; but the multiplicity of his meetings, his air of pained disgust (reminding her vaguely of the Salvation Army), and habitual depression, left no doubt as to their general righteousness. His cause, whatever it might be, was a just one: and she saw him among the smug company of her well-to-do friends as an eagle in the barnyard. An eagle, a great kingly bird, rigged for the storms and perils of the upper air: a genius untrammeled by convention: and alongside her worshipping acquiescence she felt a strong instinctive desire to take him in hand and make him into a good citizen.

She said gently:

"Don't you get tired standing, Arnold?"

He shook his head. He was probably thinking about his ideals.

"I'd come and sit down a bit if I was you."

This time he turned and looked at the counter: then in a listless kind of way pushed off from the shutters with his shoulder and lounged across. Triumph shook her heart.

"I suppose you haven't such a thing as a cigarette on you?" inquired the idealist.

"I'm ever so sorry, Arnold, I'm afraid I haven't." Winnie felt inside her bag a second time to make sure, but it was no good. "Never mind, you can get some on the way back."

"I don't hold with Sunday opening," said Arnold.

A moment's reflection assured her that there were at least half a dozen slot machines in Kimberly Street; but with new-born diplomacy she suppressed this information and said instead:

"Well, I got a packet at home you can have, if you like. You needn't give me the money till Monday."

"Thanks," said Arnold.

"Don't mention it," said Winnie.

She moved very slightly along the counter, so that their shoulders were just touching. He didn't seem to notice. There was a looking-glass on the opposite wall, but they couldn't see themselves for a tall white object standing on the shelf below. It was shaped like a pyramid, rising steeply from its base, and as Winnie's eyes grew more accustomed to the light she made out rows of little pillars diminishing in size from the bottom upwards, where, under a flowery bell, stood a small familiar figure. . . .

"Well, I never!" exclaimed Winnie softly.

"What is it?"

"A wedding cake!"

"Well, what about it?" said Arnold, following her gaze.

"Oh, nothing. It just seemed funny, that's all."

For some minutes they continued to stare at it in silence, Winnie overwhelmed by the extraordinary coincidence. For really, it seemed as if it must be Meant. Like an Omen. No one else there but just her and Arnold and a Wedding Cake. You'd think it was enough to put ideas into any one's head. . . .

"Here, I can't wait any longer," said Arnold suddenly. "I got to get to that meeting."

And without so much as a good-by he dropped off the counter and strode out of the shop. The bread came almost immediately, but what was the use of running? It was what she'd known all along. He didn't care for girls.

III

Meanwhile the boys on the top floor, more provident than their neighbours, were breakfasting in great comfort by the gas-fire. Neither of them, however, showed any desire for conversation. To Alistair, ever on the alert for turning-points in his life, it seemed as though the meeting with Cressida might fairly count as a major crossing; but though naturally elated, he was not particularly anxious to answer questions, and so felt nothing but relief when Henry displayed a humour as taciturn as his own. In silence they heated coffee, cut bread, and passed each other marmalade. With an occasional monosyllable Henry assumed his plus-fours and left the house; nor did Alistair give another thought to his behaviour until at least two hours later, when he overtook old Ma Parker on the stairs.

She remarked, with a rheumy ogle, that he had not been long in finding out the pleasures of the town.

"Three o'clock in the morning!" cackled the old lady. "You'll be a regular all-nighter before long."

Alistair was startled to detect a definite note of congratulation in the aged voice, and with a youthful lack of judgment decided to correct her.

"It was exactly two when I turned out the landing light," he mentioned. "I heard the church clock."

"Oh, well, it must 'ave been your friend, then. Woke me right out of me sleep, 'e did, kicking against the stairs. I just kept awake long enough to 'ear 'im past my Winnie's door, and that's when *I* 'eard the clock too."

In the first flutter of outraged modesty Alistair had scarcely time to be surprised by this unexpected light on his friend's habits; but as soon as he was once more alone the information became very interesting indeed. It was, he decided, quite possible that Henry had not been there when he himself came in. Across a large and darkened room one might easily mistake a heap of blankets for a recumbent friend, and Alistair tried to remember whether they had made their beds that morning. Very likely not, for he personally had merely wriggled into some loose coverings and gone to sleep.

So Henry too had undressed in the dark. Henry too had good reason for a slight taciturnity at the breakfast-table. For Henry must have spent at least three hours in nocturnal conversation with Pooh—and of course with Christopher Robin and Eeyore as well. Thus viewed as a quartet the escapade took on a less dubious complexion; but all the same Alistair could not help thinking it rather an odd thing for Henry to have done.

For the moment, however, he had even stronger preoccupations, being possessed by an overwhelming need to write an exceptionally brilliant play immediately after lunch. The subject was still undetermined, but it was to contain a woman's part so stupendous that a young and unknown actress, creating it at the first performance, would at once take rank with Bernhardt and Ellen Terry. It seemed to Alistair that he would quite soon think of a plot if he sat down with some paper.

And in this, as it happened, he was perfectly right, for after a ham sandwich and a black coffee he returned to Number Fifteen and wrote furiously from two till half-past seven. The result was not, of course, a finished play, but rather a detailed scenario with bits of dialogue inserted at the most dramatic moments: and in the part of Jennifer Torch he had achieved, if anything, rather more than he intended. It contained all the most striking episodes of dramatic literature, including a scene on a balcony with a lover below, a scene of temporary distraction, a scene where Jennifer, having discarded her wedding-ring owing to exigencies of a gay life, sleepwalks all over London looking for it. This last was of course very spectacular, with a revolving stage, and so good that Alistair decided to shift it from the middle to the very beginning. There was also a court scene with Jennifer, disguised as a barrister, defending her own husband on a charge of murder; a scene where she rushed out of his house and slammed the door; and another, necessarily the last, wherein, having rocked her dead lover to sleep in her arms, she applied a careful make-up and took veronal. When finished it struck him, with perfect justice, as a rather unusual piece of work.

The next day he bought a two-colour ribbon and typed out a fair copy: but the day after, which should have seen him bearing it in triumph to Carey Street, Alistair's courage failed completely; and it was not till nearly a week later that he set out, in his best shirt, with the masterpiece under his arm, to dazzle Cressida.

CHAPTER IX

I

UNDER Miss Drury's name it said, "Please ring twice." With a curious mixture of emotions Alistair pressed the bell. It would be incorrect to describe him as hoping to find her out, but he was also quite definitely afraid of finding her in. For his yearning to see her was almost exactly balanced by the terror of looking a fool, and though genuinely thirsty for her voice, the sound of approaching footsteps roused nothing so much as a desire for flight. The door opened . . .

"Oh, it's you," said Cressida.

Her voice, though quite pleasant, was not markedly ecstatic, and it suddenly struck him that three o'clock was perhaps a little early for an afternoon call. He said: "I—I was just passing the end of the road, and thought I'd come and look you up. How are you?"

"Come in," said Cressida, moving back into the hall, which by daylight looked very shabby indeed. "You sound as though you've got a cold."

Alistair cleared his throat surreptitiously, and assured her it was nothing. She appeared to hesitate, and then said more cordially: "I've some friends upstairs, but they're just on the point of departure. Do come up." He followed her in, thrusting the scenario into his overcoat pocket, and remarking that he felt an awful nuisance.

"Of course you're not," said Cressida, for the first time giving him her smile. "You know how far up it is, don't you?"

The stairs were uncarpeted, and echoed their footsteps surprisingly. Cressida's were all right, a neat light clicking of French heels, but his own sounded like the tramp of an elephant. Outside her door she paused and said quickly:

"They were both in the Rep. with me at Bristol. Olga's not really a Russian."

Thus warned he made a fairly nonchalant entry and was at once introduced to the pseudo-Slav and a girl like a grey kitten. They had just been trying on each other's hats, and now appealed to Cressida for judgment.

"Doesn't mine suit her? Doesn't it, Cressida?" cried the kitten, whose name was Bobbie Day. She danced round the room in a perfect ecstasy of admiration.

"You onlee say that," observed Olga slowly, "because you lak mine bettaire. Is not that so, darrling?"

Alistair gazed in wonder. But for Cressida's warning he would have been completely deceived, she was so much more like a Russian than he would have thought possible even for a native. Her dead-black hair was parted in the center and drawn back into a tight coil: above high Mongolian cheekbones her half-closed eyes were dark with the melancholy of boundless steppes.

Even in the way she took off the hat one divined a tragic future.

"It is no good," she cried. "Take it back, Bobbee, and give me my own."

"But, darling, you're making the most awful mistake," cried Bobbie in despair. "It makes you look a dream. Cressida, do tell her she's being a perfect idiot."

"But I don't think she is," said Cressida. "Very tall women should never wear those pie-dishes. Let me look at it."

She took the hat from Olga and went to the glass, where for the next few minutes, in a series of exquisite poses, she stood adjusting the yellow saucer to its only correct angle. When this had been discovered she turned round and waited for the inevitable applause.

"My *dear*!" gasped Bobbie, "you look too marvellous! To think I've been wearing the most ravishing hat in London and never knew it!"

Olga nodded in corroboration.

"Yes, you look verree nice," she drawled. "You look lak something Chinese, only *Chinois à la rue de la Paix*. I am so jealous I would lak to kill you."

"Yes, it's good." Cressida removed the hat again and twirled it casually on one finger. "Do you really want to get rid of it, Bobbie?"

"My dear," said Bobbie frankly, "I haven't a bean in the world. I'll sell you anything I've got."

The yellow hat spun round again.

"We seem to be in the same boat," said Cressida.

"God knows how I'm going to pay the rent." She paused, while Bobbie looked hopeless and Olga generated a wave of sympathetic gloom. "I suppose you don't want a swap?"

"Not an evening cloak?" asked Bobbie suspiciously.

"Good heavens, no. I'll show you." She darted across to the divan-bed and pulled from underneath a large cardboard box. It contained a black taffeta dress with a lemon-yellow sash and long tight sleeves of the same colour.

"There!" she said triumphantly. "That's the last thing I bought before skirts got longer. But you're so short it'll be just right."

Miss Day hesitated, measuring the frock against her childish height.

"The length's all right," she said at last, "but isn't it rather—rather exaggerated?"

"You mean unusual," said Cressida, "and I should hope it is. It's a model, my dear, and I got it in Paris last time I was over."

The prospective purchaser at once turned to the neck, and there sure enough was the enticing label: "Jane-Marie, Paris."

"It's not one of the big houses," said Cressida quickly, "but all the actresses go there. They dress half the shows on the Boulevards." She took back the garment, and held it to her own shoulders with a regretful sigh. "If it wouldn't ruin the line so utterly I'd have it lengthened, but there you are. The sleeves, *on*, look like long yellow mittens . . ."

"My hat's French too," Bobbie pointed out.

"Darling, I know it is, otherwise you wouldn't have the chance of this." Cressida gazed admiringly at her reflection. "It's called 'Papillon Sage.' Isn't that charming?"

"Let me try it on," said Bobbie.

A chair scraped somewhere by the door, and looking round they saw Alistair getting up to go.

"Oh, my dear, must you?" said Cressida absently, still holding Le Papillon Sage.

"'Fraid I must," replied Alistair, "I've got to meet a man at four." Miss Day was already busy with hooks and eyes, but Olga extended her hand as though for a loyal kiss, and he took pleasure in shaking it vigorously.

"You'll forgive my not coming downstairs, won't you?" murmured Cressida; and gathering up the folds of taffeta she held them ready to slip over Bobbie's head.

II

It was obviously impossible ever to see her again.

In this conviction Alistair lived heart-broken for the next fortnight. It was lucky that Henry, as term progressed, had become completely absorbed in student life, so that the behavior of his friend, though effortlessly traditional, now passed unnoticed. He did once, indeed, offer the loan of some fruit salts, but in general Alistair might sigh, moan, and toss unsleeping without attracting the least attention. This state of affairs continued, as has been stated, for two weeks, at the end of which period the original sentence was slightly modified.

It was obviously impossible ever to call again.

On this slender allowance of hope Alistair's spirits at once began to revive. His existence, no longer aimless, took on a totally different complexion; and one of the first results was a sudden craving for the society of Pooh, Eeyore, and Christopher Robin. This was of course inevitable, since though he could meet Cressida in Carey Street every day of the week, it was doubtful whether such encounters would give the desired impression of being completely casual. In the sitting-room of Christopher Robin, however, there could be no suspicion of pre-arrangement, and thither Alistair now began to make his way as often as possible. Henry, fortunately a frequent visitor, was never allowed to go unaccompanied, and once or twice he even ventured to call on his own account; but except for a slight fluttering of maiden interest, the visits were fruitless. A second reading (of *Mary Rose*, by Sir J.M. Barrie) roused him to the most feverish anticipation, only to be followed by such blackness of despair that he at last resorted to the method of oblique inquiry.

"I tell you who wasn't there," he remarked to Henry (they had left together, this time), "that girl in black who read Lady Fidget."

Henry reflected a moment.

"No more she was," he agreed at last. "Eeyore did tell me her name—something a bit odd."

"I thought she read rather well."

"I didn't," said Henry. They walked on a few yards in silence, and then, as though feeling his dictum needed expanding, added: "After all, we weren't supposed to be *acting*. She's been on the stage, you know."

"Evidently," said Alistair, suppressing the natural impulse to tell Henry what a fool he was.

"Of course," Henry continued, with an air of summing up and dismissing the whole question, "they don't know her very well."

"Really?" said Alistair, very much surprised. "Somehow I got the impression she half lived there."

"Lord, no. Look here, if you don't mind, I'd like to take the tube at Baker Street. There's a nail in my left boot."

As a result of this conversation Alistair at once retired from social life and took to going long walks in Kensington Gardens. In this he showed unintentionally good sense, for the exercise, coupled with the brisk air and a smell of bonfires, could not fail to do him a great deal of good. The green banks of the Serpentine were already sprinkled with early seagulls, and in the contemplation of these engaging fowl, no less than in tramping through the crackle of fallen leaves, Alistair's spirits began to regain their normal enthusiasm. (He even attempted in an expansive moment, to convey something of his emotion to old Henry.

"Those gulls," he reported, "are perfectly exquisite—the daintiest things you can imagine. One would never think, to look at them, that they spend the summer beating up and down the North Sea."

"Most of them don't," said Henry. "Most of them never beat farther than the nearest sewage farm.")

As time went on Alistair's knowledge of the ground approached that of a park-keeper, but in spite of increasing familiarity he never ceased to be struck by the amount of free entertainment to be enjoyed therein. Hand-fed squirrels were a commonplace, sparrows haloed the feet of innumerable Saints Francis, and on one occasion he observed, without much surprise, a large grey monkey clambering about the naked branches of a chestnut. It was attached to some ten yards of chain, at the other end of which a lady sat reading the *Morning Post* and exchanging remarks with interested bystanders. Alistair halted just long enough to learn that the monkey was a feminine one and came from Madagascar, and passed on towards the Round Pond.

It was a brilliantly fine November morning, cold enough to make gloved fingers tingle, and with more sunshine than colour in the pale-blue sky. Alistair walked faster and faster, delight in his own motion overcoming even the delight of watching two sawyers at work in an oak-tree. The Gardens were settling down for the winter, and were no longer a spot for loiterers. Already the iron chairs were folded and stacked in long rows, their seats and legs so closely fitted as to remind him of those barbaric dances in which a whole naked tribe, packed belly to back like so many sardines, sways and stamps in a writhing Indian file.

"I'd like to describe that somewhere," thought Alistair.

Another hundred yards took him to the margin of the pond, where there were more seagulls riding at anchor among the usual squadrons of ducks. In spite of the fine day (or perhaps because it was getting on for lunch-time) there was no one in sight save one small boy, a ragged urchin of about eight years old with a white scut of shirt appearing through his knickers. But no mere sartorial error could mar the general effect as he stood, gazing dispassionately over the water, in an attitude of easy nonchalance that would have won the approval of a Chesterfield. One hand rested lightly on his hip, from the other depended an ingenious stone-carrier made of knotted string and containing a good-sized stone.

"Hello, son," said Alistair rashly.

The urchin's head turned slowly round to the exact point at which he could see his interlocutor from the tail of his left eye; and having done so, as slowly returned. It was the cut direct.

Hotly denying his mortification, Alistair nevertheless began to stride smartly round the margin of the pond. There were more people on the other side (it was quite possible, he reflected, that the small boy had driven every one away), including several yachtsmen; and here his annoyance was sufficiently abated to permit him to linger and look at the boats. The water was covered with bobbing seagulls, and as he watched a sudden impulse—rumour of food, enemy or the wind—swept them up in whirling flight. For an instant the air for three feet above the surface was filled with a pattern of wings, and in that same instant a yacht with royal-blue sails swept proudly through them and grounded at Alistair's feet.

It was so beautiful that he remembered Cressida.

All the more bitter because he had forgotten for an hour, all the sweeter because of birds and a blue ship, love returned and shook his heart. Her image was in the sight of his eyes; her name was the blood drumming in his ears.

But now he could bear the Gardens no longer, and for the next few days turned instead towards the City of London, within whose crowded limits he discovered many ten-mile walks. Saturday afternoon was one of the best times, for then there was more room to stride blindly along the pavement; and it was on one of these occasions that Alistair, returning along the Strand, was surprised by the sight of Winnie Parker in the queue for Ibsen's *Ghosts*.

CHAPTER X

I

"HELLO," said Winnie, "where did you spring from?" She was wearing a new pink mackintosh, with Russian boots to match, and a sort of black velvet jockey cap tied in a bow on top. Securing this bow was a small paste ornament in the shape of Mickey Mouse, which Alistair recognized as the offering of Charlie Coe, and her appearance was further brightened by a large buttonhole of artificial orchids. The rest of the queue was composed largely of spectacled young women, many of them carrying the text of the play.

"Hello," said Alistair. "I didn't think this was your sort of show."

"Why, what is it?" Winnie stepped back and looked up at the posters. "Coo. I never heard of it. Is it a thriller?"

"In its way. But didn't you even know what you were going to see?"

"Oh, I wasn't going *in*," said Winnie, now stepping out of her place and joining him on the curb. "I was just standing there to eat my lunch. It's too cold now in the parks." And she indicated a crumpled paper bag lying in the gutter.

"I see," said Alistair, noting afresh her extreme skinniness. "Which way are you going now?"

"Up there." She nodded vaguely in the direction of Oxford Circus, but seemed loath to give further particulars. "Where've you been yourself?"

"Oh, just taking a bit of exercise." After a morning's solitary brooding the prospect of her company was suddenly attractive, and by common consent they fell into step and began to walk up the Charing Cross Road, Winnie's costume drawing many admiring glances from old and young.

With regular feeding, he told himself, sideways-glancing at her pert features, she might be really pretty: the delicate childish line from ear to chin was charming. It was only when he tried to visualize her as the happy product of a healthy environment that he realized how essential a part of her charm was that very Cockney fragility. Under-nourishment had been so constant a factor in her life that a well-fed Winnie became at once quite a different person; and though the paper-bag régime was to be deplored it did somehow seem to produce the maximum artistic good. Curious. He looked at her again, trotting beside him in those incredible pink boots, and marvelled at the tenacity which informed her small body. That line of the jaw—had he called it childish? It was firm as a rock. That ingenuous, china-blue gaze—what better defence against all other eyes? Behind the rather pretty, rather badly-painted mask lay a power of resistance beside which his own intelligent resolution was as straw to granite. Nothing, save possibly a motor accident, would ever be too much for her: faced by the utmost disasters of civilized life she would square those narrow shoulders and somehow see the thing through: not necessarily in silence, shrilling probably to the four winds, clawing right and left for a foothold; but surviving in the end.

"I bet you don't know where I'm going," said Winnie, unable to keep it in a moment longer.

"Buckingham Palace?"

"Funny!" She walked a few more steps, then turned to watch the effect. "An audition."

"What's that?"

"Well! And I thought you knew everything. It means a try-out for chorus-girls," said Winnie. "I saw it in the paper."

It was of course inevitable, as soon as one came to think of it, that she should want to go on the stage; but somehow Alistair was unprepared. She had always seemed so contented, so eminently pleased with herself and her surroundings: nor had she, so far as he was aware, any marked histrionic talent.

"I didn't know you sang," he said curiously.

"I don't, not so as you'd notice. But I can dance all right."

That he could well believe. She was as light as a feather.

"And I've got nice legs," Winnie pointed out. "You can't see them now because of these boots, but every one says so."

"Personally I always thought they were a bit too thin," said Alistair, who was beginning to be really interested.

"That's the modern taste. In *Beautiful Woman* it says the slender Greek ideal has returned to unite Art and Fashion. Besides, I expect I could put on a bit of weight if I tried."

Alistair agreed heartily. He had an idea that, like a jockey, she would gain whole pounds from one glass of port. "Only be sure you don't put it on in the wrong place, or you'll never get in the front row."

They had by this time reached Cambridge Circus, and here Winnie stopped and gave him her hand. She was now quite near her destination, she said, and wanted to go and have a final tidy-up; so with many good wishes Alistair watched her trot off down Shaftesbury Avenue and in five minutes had forgotten she existed.

Inside his head a dialogue was going on (as it had been for days) between a Very Great Man, who looked a little like Henry Montague, and a youthful genius who looked exactly like Alistair. The great man had just put down the draft of Jennifer Torch and now remarked, in a surprised voice, "But can it really be, my dear boy, that this is your first play?"

"Oh, rather," said Alistair.

"And you say you have three others of the same calibre waiting to be written?"

"At least."

Henry Montague took off his glasses and turned to Cressida. (She had been there all the time, of course, but just sitting still and admiring.) "Then let me tell you, Miss Drury, that your fiancé is a very remarkable young man. In fact, if it hadn't become such a cliché"—he broke off while they all crossed New Oxford Street—"I should be inclined to use that long-suffering word genius."

For perhaps ten minutes, with these glorious words ringing in his ears, Alistair walked on air. Itinerant flower-sellers marked him from afar, organ-grinders held out their hats with confiding gestures: for here (they thought) comes a young man who has received good news. But they were all disappointed, for before he had become sufficiently reckless to part with a copper his triumphant mood collapsed, and the pavement-artist at the next corner did not spare him a second glance.

"But it'll never happen," thought Alistair desperately, "it'll never happen to me. Nothing ever does. If I had the guts of a rabbit I'd stop a 'bus and finish with it. I don't matter to any one."

The pathos of such a situation was almost more than he could bear: it might be days, he reflected, before the police even succeeded in identifying his body. He pulled out his pocket-book to see if it contained his name or address, and found it empty save for some slips of paper on which he had intended to jot down interesting thoughts. They were fortunately still blank, and stepping into a doorway he took a pencil and wrote two messages. One was to the police, and said, "Please tell Henry Brough, 15 Bloom Street, Paddington. ALISTAIR FRENCH"; the other, to Henry: "Please break the news to Aunt Gertrude." Looking them over he wished he had put "inform" instead of "tell"; but at any rate they were quite plain, and he came out of the doorway fully prepared for sudden death.

But there was now, ironically enough, hardly any traffic at all, for without thinking of his direction Alistair had been bearing steadily northwards, and now found himself in a quiet thoroughfare of grey houses and leafless plane trees. It had an air of Bloomsbury, and looking up for the name he saw that he was in Carey Street.

This fresh evidence of the power of love was so overwhelming that he had to accept the support of a lamp-post: and behold, it was the lamp-post outside Cressida's dwelling. The next movement should obviously have been a triumphant storming of the citadel and possible abduction; but here Alistair's courage failed. By giving himself time to think he gave himself time to fear, and above all to remember the unfortunate circumstances of his last visit. Olga returned to paralyze his will, the yellow hat still made a fool of him. . . .

For perhaps half an hour he stood there, gazing up through the gathering dusk: then suddenly a light appeared in the top window, a yellow patch quickly masked by the drawing of a curtain, and he knew that Cressida was there. She had been sitting in the dark, as he himself so often sat in Bloom Street, weaving proud dreams and feeling a little lonely. . . . The picture was so sweet and unalarming that Alistair almost rang the bell; but the image of Olga was still too potent, and instead he remained where he was, hurling a hundred prayers at Fortune and exercising his will-power to its fullest extent. He willed that she should look out and see him and come down and let him in.

"Cressida, Cressida—"

At that moment, like an answering miracle, the top window was thrown up and the curtain drawn aside. Unable, even by cricking his neck, to see if it were she, Alistair stepped backwards off the pavement and was knocked down by a cruising taxi.

II

His first emotion, as he picked himself from the gutter, was one of pure disgust at not having been severely injured. Apart from the wasted notes, he had missed an unrivaled opportunity. A broken leg, a fractured skull, and they must have carried him into the house, there to die in Cressida's arms: but the collision taking place at barely three miles an hour he had sustained no more damage than a muddied coat and a shaking. With a sudden access of ineffectual pedestrian anger he picked up his hat and flourished it violently at the retreating cab.

"Here, look where you're going, can't you?" he called.

Seeing him uninjured, the driver merely shouted back something in the nature of a *tu quoque* which Alistair decided to ignore. The mud was still too wet to brush off, and a growing stiffness cramped his left shoulder; but in spite of these disadvantages he felt considerably less miserable than before. It struck him that even with a cracked skull they would hardly have carried him right up to the top floor: he began to feel almost pleased at being still alive, and almost a hero for the way he had blackguarded the cabby. Number Fifteen, too, would be thrilled and expansive over his narrow escape—they always liked to hear of accidents to people they knew; and in planning the recital of his adventure Alistair unthinkingly turned out of Carey Street and started to walk home. The incident had, in fact, cheered him up enormously.

CHAPTER XI

I

IT WAS Alistair's bad luck to return and find Number Fifteen, usually so interested in street accidents, already provided with a far more exciting topic. Henry, indeed, offered to brush his coat on him, as soon as the mud should have dried, but every one else was completely taken up with the affair of Winnie and the chorus-girl.

It all arose, naturally enough, from the fateful audition. On reaching the theatre Winnie had found a mob of some fifty or sixty young women waiting outside the stage door. It was still nearly forty minutes to the appointed hour, so she took her place on the outskirts of the throng and began to pass the time by examining her fellow-aspirants; as a result of which inspection she very sensibly decided to go home.

("Smart!" said Winnie, recounting her experience on a subsequent occasion. "They fairly knocked you over. I thought first I'd got into the wrong queue, and we was all going to see the King. It was no place for me")

Just as she was leaving, however, a girl who had been standing against the wall suddenly crumpled up and slid to her knees on the pavement. Winnie naturally stopped, helped her up again, and upon inquiry found that she had not eaten since the previous morning. They then went to tea at a Maison Lyons.

It was at this point that Winnie's benevolence, in the opinion of Number Fifteen, definitely ran away with her. It was quite right to assist the young lady to her feet and feed her with ham sandwiches: but she had no call to bring her home to sleep.

"But don't I tell you she hadn't a ruddy cent?" demanded Winnie fiercely. "What d'you expect me to do—book her a room at the Ritz?"

(It was the following morning, and the subject was being freely canvassed on all landings while Nina—for such was the young lady's name—had her sleep out on Winnie's bed.)

"Now, now, there's no need to use language," said Mrs. Griffin reprovingly.

"Well, go on then, some one, tell me what I should've done," snapped Winnie.

In the hall below Charlie Coe looked expressively at Mr. Hickey and Mr. Hickey looked back at Charlie Coe. They both knew quite well what she could have done, but neither, in the face of those blazing blue eyes, had the nerve to say it. She was quite capable of throwing things. . . .

"Has she got her unemployment card?" asked Arnold Comstock, who had been following the discussion from the door of his room.

"Oh, my Gawd, how d'you s'pose *I* know?" asked the exasperated rescuer. "She's been out of work two years, off and on . . ."

Again Charlie and Mr. Hickey exchanged glances. It was just what they expected. Overcome by his feelings Charlie nearly exchanged a glance with Arnold as well, but quickly turned it into a glare of contempt.

"And whatever Ma'll say I'm sure *I* don't know," continued the gloating accents of Mrs. Griffin.

"Ma'll say whatever I do," flashed Winnie. "She likes young company, Ma does. And if I like to let her sleep in my room I don't see it's any one's business to say I can't. I don't see what you're all gassin' about, truly I don't."

"That's all right, my dear," interposed Mr. Hickey. "We only don't want to see you put upon . . ." He looked at Charlie, but Charlie was holding his tongue: and there the argument might have ended had not a new voice now joined in the deliberations.

"How long," inquired the new voice thoughtfully, "is she likely to stay?"

It was Henry Brough, leaning from the very top landing of all, and they looked up in grateful surprise. He had put his finger, it was felt, on the exact spot.

"Till she gets another job, o' course," said Winnie.

Henry thought a bit.

"I believe there's an awful lot of unemployment in the theatre—"

"It's something crool," corroborated Mrs. Griffin. "One of my ladies 'as been out eight months."

"She did ought to have an unemployment card," said Arnold Comstock.

"Honest, Win," added Charlie earnestly, "you don't know what you may be letting yourself in for. Why, she mayn't be a—"

But Winnie had stood them long enough. In any case, her mind was made up, so why discuss the matter further?

"You make me sick, the whole boiling of you," she said briefly.

Her withering glance swept the staircase from top to bottom; she uttered a vulgar ejaculation suggestive of nausea; and the next instant the whole house was shaken by the slamming of the Parker door.

There was a short pause, heavy with discomfort and a vague sense of injury. So must the friends of St. Francis have felt, when he persisted in bringing home so very many animals.

"You can't do nothing at all," said Mr. Hickey.

II

He was quite correct. Winnie had her way, and Nina continued to inhabit Number Fifteen, sleeping in her hostess's bed and eating at the Parker board. Every morning after breakfast she set off, gorgeously attired, to visit the agents, and returned with unfailing punctuality about half-past six. This made a very tiring day of it, and Winnie, who got in at much the same hour, was constantly urging her to take a rest. So until supper Nina rested, generally with her feet up on a chair; but afterwards, if any one were going to the pictures, she would make sufficient effort to accompany the party. Once or twice, Nina being said to crave refined society, Alistair and Henry were asked down for the evening, and afterwards spent a good deal of time discussing her type.

"I always thought chorus-girls were supposed to be attractive," said Henry glumly.

Alistair looked at his friend with a slight feeling of superiority. Old Henry might smoke caporal all day, but his standard of feminine beauty would still be the chocolate box. It took a man of experience to appreciate (for instance) the greenish shadow in buttercup-yellow locks. . . .

"There's something funny about her hair," proceeded Henry. "It looks as though it's been dyed, or something." He paused, not without a certain coquettishness. "Did you notice how she kept on calling me darling?"

"She called every one darling," replied Alistair rather unkindly. "For two pins she'd have sat on your knee as well." A warmly affectionate address was indeed the keynote of Nina's personality. She stroked, she patted, she caressed: with the slightest encouragement she would also have nestled and twined, particularly about the manly bulk of Eddie Cribb; but the atmosphere of a Parker soirée was scarcely favourable to serious necking. "She's one of those women," finished Alistair thoughtfully, "who never look quite natural in a chair."

Winnie, meanwhile, was tasting the sweets of female friendship for the first time; and as Alistair listened to her Platonic *épanchements* it struck him that she was passing belated through an emotional Fourth Form. She adored Nina with the whole-hearted passion usually reserved for games-mistresses alone, and even developed a mild contempt for great rough boys like Charlie Coe. More astonishing still, she began to have a slight look of Nina, imitating as far as possible her languorous walk, melting glances, and general make-up. The first two attributes gave her considerable trouble, but a lipstick could be duplicated at the nearest Woolworth's; and soon Winnie's pallid cheeks and sooty eyelids were drawing anxious inquiries from customers and friends.

"You want either," said Charlie Coe impartially, "to take some off or put some on. It doesn't matter which, but just now you look like a corpse."

"I'd rather look like a corpse than a kipper," retorted Winnie. "Every time I look at you I smell the sea."

"What *she* wants is some good underwear," put in Mrs. Griffin. (The conversation was as usual taking place on the landing, where the constant *va-et-vient* made one peculiarly liable to such interruptions.) "No wonder she looks perished, with no more protection than a bit of lace."

To Winnie's fury Charlie decided to take the matter up.

"Don't you really wear no more than that?" he asked anxiously.

"You take my word for it," said Mrs. Griffin. "I see 'er washing 'anging up every Sunday."

Charlie's concern deepened.

"Look here, Win," he said, "you're not to go playing about with your health this time of year. You ought to wear wool. What've you got on under that jumper-thing, f'rinstance?"

But for the first time in her life words failed her. With an inarticulate cry Winnie rushed to the sitting-room door and flung it open.

"Ma!" she screamed. "Here's Charlie Coe wants to see me underclothes!"

There was a short silence, followed by a sound of shuffling footsteps, and old Ma Parker appeared in the doorway. She said:

And when she had finished Charlie Coe was nowhere to be seen.

III

On the lumpy ottoman at the foot of her bed Winnie lay staring into the dark. It was not the lumps, however, that kept her awake, but the pleasures of imagination. Benevolence welled to overflowing as she watched the sleeping figure of her protegee. A hundred charming plans flitted through her brain, all based on an everlasting friendship between herself and the girl on the bed. They would open mutual hearts, shave each others' necks, go shopping on Thursday afternoons. They might even—and here Winnie could hardly lie still for excitement—dress exactly alike! It couldn't have been more than a week ago she had seen two girls in the Park, two girls just about the same age as her and Nina, dressed in bright green coats and little green hats with white feathers. Ever so nice they'd looked—and the attention they attracted! There must have been at least five or six boys strolling along behind. Against the dark wall Winnie projected a beautiful moving picture of herself and her friend, sauntering airily across Hyde Park, and attired in identical coats of . . .

. . . Of bright red cloth with leopard collars.

"Cool," thought Winnie. "We wouldn't half make 'em sit up!"

In spite of the lumps she fairly wriggled with joy as she planned to go and ask at the shop the very next day. Madame Louise could easy make another, though goodness knew when they would be able to pay for it. . . . If only, thought Winnie, if only Nina was earning *something*, they wouldn't have a care in the world. Why, she could live at Bloom Street for practically nothing, sharing the room like that and all eating together. If only she could have just pocket-money even, because after all the food didn't make so much difference. . . .

"Why, I eat enough for ten meself," thought Winnie, mentally puffing her slim body to the size of a barrel. "If I don't look out I'll be getting fat as butter." The Riviera, too—it wasn't exactly dear, considering what you got, but it was more than you wanted. All right for Charlie and Mr. Hickey, who had their strength to keep up. . . .

She turned over, cautiously, so as not to twang the springs, and pulled the miscellaneous bedclothes well over her head. A great contentment warmed her heart. It would soon be tomorrow.

CHAPTER XII

I

ON THE following Saturday Mr. Horner had arranged to take a small group to view the backside of the elephant on the Albert Memorial. The party was to consist, according to Henry, of only the very best people, and Alistair might therefore consider himself definitely flattered at receiving an invitation.

Alistair listened, wavering. He was just about to embark on the most exciting twenty-four hours of his whole life, but having no gift of prophecy merely remarked that, on the whole, he thought he would rather stay at home.

"Oh, come along," said Henry robustly. "It's a nice crisp afternoon, and the walk will do you good."

It now occurred to Alistair, though he was too proud to ask, that Cressida might just possibly be of the party; and the hope, however faint, was sufficient to make him take down his hat and coat. Otherwise he did not anticipate the least enjoyment, and the sight of the group assembled at Marble Arch merely confirmed his pessimism. Miss Drury being absent, they all looked like hell.

II

The party, numbering about fifteen in all, set off in a straggling crocodile. At the head marched Mr. Horner, flanked by two admiring wits and unbearably picturesque in his black jersey; next came Henry, Eeyore and Christopher

Robin, all very bright and hearty; then a bunch of miscellaneous disciples, male and female; and finally Alistair, sulkily bringing up the rear with two plain young women who chattered about history. One could tell they were very up in their subject because instead of saying James the First and Charles the Second they said Jimmy One and Charlie Two.

Once arrived at the Memorial, however, the situation, from being unpleasant, became definitely poisonous. A cursory glance satisfied Alistair that the backside of the elephant was exactly what might have been expected from a Victorian sculptor: that is to say, it precisely resembled an elephant's backside; but Mr. Horner insisted on mounting the topmost step and delivering a mock-heroic speech on its implicit affinity with the Indian Love Lyrics, while the rest of the party stood grouped below in tripperish attitudes.

It was more than Alistair could bear. The wind was sharp, the passers-by naturally interested. He went round to the other side of the Memorial and sat down on the steps.

He had not been there more than five minutes when a pair of neat brown boots halted beside him, and a voice said politely:

"I beg your pardon, but haven't we met before?"

III

Alistair looked up and saw a light-brown overcoat, a brown-and-white check scarf, and a pleasantly tanned face with mutton-chop whiskers. It was the man at the Embryo Club.

Eagerly he scrambled to his feet and acknowledged the acquaintance. He also added that his name was Alistair French.

"And mine's Raymond Paget. This is very amusing. Let me see, it *was* at the Embryo, wasn't it?"

Alistair flushed slightly and explained that he was not a member.

"My dear fellow, no more am I. No one one meets again ever is. It just happens to be one of those places where everybody in London is seen once in their lives. I think their aunts must take them . . ." He paused, as though considering this point; then said kindly: "Unless you want to sit down again, why not stroll along with me? It's not so cold walking."

The invitation was irresistible, but Alistair, fearing pursuit, or at any rate friendly cries, from the group by the elephant, took good care that they descended on the same side. He did not want to have to dissociate himself from any more backgrounds.

As they proceeded towards Kensington he learnt that his companion was a painter, specializing in portraits but occasionally dabbling in landscape for his own pleasure. He also appeared to command considerable means, but whether from purely artistic sources Alistair could not quite make out. The life glimpsed through his conversation, however, was definitely not that of a fanatic: winters on the Riviera, trips to Norway, passing allusions to London celebrities, all mingled very naturally with the descriptions of pictures. He also talked very intelligently about the young, and how there sometimes seemed to be a point at which one could do by instinct what later one could not do by technique. Almost the best thing he had ever done, said Mr. Paget, was a little sketch of two trees at Versailles, when he was quite a youngster. It hung in his studio at the very moment, the only picture on four walls; and he had never painted anything since to make him take it down.

"I'd like to see it," said Alistair, speaking almost for the first time.

"Well, why not?" said Mr. Paget. "Come and have a drink at my studio. It's quite near."

"This is real," thought Alistair, "this is happening to me. It is what I always knew would happen, once I got away." Aloud he said:

"That's most awfully good of you. I should love to." They went out through the nearest gate and halted by a 'bus stop. This was mere accident, however, and no indication of their proposed mode of transport. Mr. Paget looked once up and down the road, remarked that it was getting dark early, and hailed a taxi.

IV

"Not a bad little hole," said Raymond Paget, taking off his overcoat and revealing a coquettish yellow pullover.

Alistair liked the studio very much indeed. It was a large square room on the ground-floor, simply furnished with two divans and the apparatus of cocktail-making. His host at once mixed a good supply of dry Martini and sat down with his feet up, instructing Alistair to nose round until he was tired and then do likewise. Most of his canvases, he said, were unfortunately packed away, but there were one or two portfolios somewhere in the corner . . . only on second thoughts he wouldn't advise his young friend to bother with those, they were full of old working sketches, of no interest to any one save the artist.

"Look at those two trees there," he counseled, "and you'll see the best bit of painting I ever did in my life. Sunlight and leaves—what more does any one want?"

Alistair liked the picture very much indeed. It was a charming thing, twelve square inches of airy colour that was also two slender trees bending before the wind. It looked as though it had been painted very quickly, all in an afternoon, and by a young man in love. Possibly owing to the cocktail, he made this last observation aloud.

"Quite right," said Mr. Paget, "I was. There's nothing like love for landscapes." He, too, stared thoughtfully at the painting, apparently lost in tender recollection, while Alistair drifted back to the other sofa. He had plenty of recollections of his own, if it came to that, but he preferred to review them sitting down.

"I remember—" began Mr. Paget.

So did Alistair. He remembered with sudden, astonishing vividness, the curve of Cressida's cheek as she stood pulling on her glove. By closing his eyes he could see it quite clearly against the dark paint of Pooh's door: and no artist had ever drawn anything half so beautiful.

"Her *sister's* name," continued Mr. Paget dreamily, "was Louise . . . or something similar; but I'll tell you that part later."

Her eyes, thought Alistair, her grey eyes that smiled so much more readily than her lips; and the sweet turn of her neck as she tried a yellow hat before the glass: she was the loveliest thing in all the world, and he would never see her again. . . . With the finishing of his drink a terrible melancholy assailed him, and he gladly accepted Mr. Paget's advice to have one or two more. He had, in point of fact, three. The studio was very warm, his host's voice low and soothing; and it presently struck him that if he put his head right down on the cushions the light would no longer be in his eyes. This new position proved a great success, enabling him to think of Cressida with so little distraction that within ten minutes reverie had merged into dreaming and Alistair was fast asleep.

. . . And presently, in his dream, he found himself walking along a broad, snowy road that wound beside a frozen river. It was very cold, and his muffled footfall made no impression on the brooding silence. Every now and then he stopped to look back, for he was expecting to be overtaken by a fellow-traveller: but the road stretched empty behind him. It seemed to straighten out, too, as he passed, because he could see right to the horizon, whereas in front there was always a bend cutting off the view, and the river ran between narrow gorges of snow-covered rock. The only colour in the landscape was the purplish-silver of the reeds that grew thickly along either bank, each stem casting its separate shadow on the smooth ice. There was no snow upon the river, though upon the road it lay six inches deep, and, being of the consistency of icing-sugar, closed up evenly after every step; which was an additional source of worry, since he could not be quite sure that his companion was not already ahead.

Overcome by anxiety, Alistair stopped again and scanned the flat white plain. It was melancholy travelling alone, but the blind road called him; and he was just about to set off again when suddenly, not on the road where he had expected her, but on the frozen river, a girl skimmed past and disappeared round the next curve. It was all over in a second, he had only time to catch a glimpse of dark furs framing a white cheek, and she was gone forever.

Gone forever. . . .

V

He woke up to find his host still talking, but also with the impression of having slept for a considerable length of time; and this was confirmed when Mr. Paget, who had hitherto shown no signs of fatigue, suddenly broke off to announce a craving for refreshment.

"Come and have dinner with me," he invited. "There's a little place just round the corner—undistinguished but handy. The food isn't bad." He removed his legs from the sofa and stood up.

Not entirely without a suspicion that it was still a part of his dream, Alistair accepted the invitation and followed suit. The floor was a trifle uneven, but only for the first step or two, and the cold air outside did him so much good that by the time they reached the restaurant he was able to walk quite without thinking. Though completely unpretentious, Angelotti's was so far superior to the Riviera as to give them rolls and butter without being asked, and Alistair also noticed that the waiter—no Clara, but a dapper youth in regulation dress—took an order for Chianti without any show of surprise.

But even wine could not entirely renew Mr. Paget's flow of conversation, and with the arrival of the sweet the word passed to his young friend. Alistair was only too pleased to take it, for the alliance of Chianti and dry Martini had done even more than was expected of them; and with the very slightest of connections—a reference to the architecture of the Middle Temple—he plunged into a detailed account of his great play.

Mr. Paget listened with considerable interest, due at first (it must be admitted) to the mistaken belief that Jennifer Torch was a real person, a girl with whom this excitable young lad seemed to have been extraordinarily intimate; but even after realizing the error his interest was scarcely abated.

"You must send me the whole thing," he declared over his coffee. "It sounds damned unusual. I know a lot of theatrical folk—"

In Alistair's eye there began to shine a new and purposeful light.

"I suppose," he hazarded, "an outsider has about as much chance of getting his play read as of swimming the Channel?"

"My dear boy!" His host's eyebrows flew up in protest. "*Don't* tell me you too have got hold of that idiotic idea! Why, half the leading actresses in London are literally screaming for new stuff. You send your play along to me, and if I think it has possibilities I'll get one of 'em to read it."

There was a short but impressive silence. Then Alistair gripped the seat of his chair with both hands and said boldly:

"Look here, if you can wait half an hour I'll go and get it now."

Mr. Paget looked at him thoughtfully, then at the clock. It was a quarter to nine.

"Right," he said. "Come straight back to the studio and you'll find me there."

Alistair gulped down what was left of his coffee and rushed from the restaurant. He was in such a state of excitement that he turned the wrong way and had hurried fifty yards before realizing his mistake. This necessitated his running all the way back past the restaurant again (where Mr. Paget, still seated in the window, was greatly surprised to see him flash by) and into the tube station by the Exit Only. Here he found he had nothing less (and indeed nothing more) than a two-shilling piece, and was forced to stand fuming while the man juggled with coppers and the train roared in below. At last he got his ticket, was nearly bisected by the sliding doors, thrust them back just in time, and fell into a corner seat.

All the other passengers looked at him with interest, many quite pleased to know that the doors did not actually kill one. His immediate neighbour, a pretty girl in a blue hat, also glanced from time to time round the edge of her *Mirror*; but Alistair had no thoughts for anything beyond the next stage of his journey. That was the two or three hundred yards between Kimberly Street Station and the top of Bloom Street, and he could not make up his mind whether it would be quicker to take a 'bus or go on foot. Henry said it was quicker on a 'bus, but that was if you caught one without any waiting, and if you didn't get caught in the traffic . . . running was probably safer in the end.

So Alistair ran once more, twisting like a football player through the Saturday evening crowd. He reached Number Fifteen in just under ten minutes, let himself in, rushed upstairs, discovered Henry embracing a young lady by firelight, hastily lit the gas, rummaged through his papers, found what he wanted, turned out the gas again, and rushed back to Kensington.

"You look hot," said Mr. Paget sympathetically. "Have a drink."

Alistair nodded and reached for the glass. There was neither breath nor moisture left in his body.

Raymond Paget mixed another for himself, and returned to the sofa. It was evident that he had shortened the time of waiting quite successfully, and was now even more mellow than before. Once or twice he sang a little, pleasantly, something about "Let us take the road, I hear the sound of coaches"; but his intelligence was as acute as ever, and he had really very little difficulty in remembering who Alistair probably was.

"Have another," he urged cordially. . . .

"No, thanks awfully," said Alistair. He couldn't remember quite how much he had had to drink that evening, but it was beginning to feel enough, and he wanted a clear head for his play. "Would you like to hear my stuff now?"

"I can imagine nothing more perfect," replied Raymond Paget dreamily, "than to lie here with a whisky-and-soda listening to a young poet read his works."

"It isn't poetry, you know," said Alistair, with a touch of anxiety. "It's a play."

Mr. Paget waved his glass.

"When I said 'poetry,' I meant it symbolically. Personally I would much rather it were a play. Now begin." Diffidently at first, but with growing enthusiasm, Alistair embarked on his vast scenario. It was so long since he had looked at the thing that many of the episodes struck him as being even better than he remembered them, and this lent an added conviction to his delivery. Indeed, of all art-forms, the scenario is probably the easiest to recite aloud, given a little imagination on the part of the reader. All he has to do is to keep an eye on the cross-headings and give full rein to his descriptive prose. In this way the sleep-walking, the door-slamming, the court-scene, the veronal, all went with a triumphant swing that brought Mr. Paget bouncing to his feet in genuine amazement.

"But, my dear boy," he cried, as soon as Alistair had come to the end, "do you realize that you've done a very remarkable thing? It's got breadth, it's got vision, it's got scale! As for the leading woman's part, of course that's in a class by itself. What a chance! It's the sort of part actresses spend their whole lives looking for—though, mind you, there are precious few nowadays who could get away with it." He paused, his face suddenly convulsed as by some vital emotion, then smote the mantelpiece so that their glasses rattled.

"Camilla Dane!" cried Mr. Paget.

"Camilla Dane?" repeated Alistair, equally prepared to smite things on the slightest provocation. "Isn't she in revue?"

"That's right. But she's tired of it. She wants to go into straight, and she's looking for a play to do it in. Because when she says straight she doesn't mean Ibsen. It's got to be something spectacular (that's where your opening comes in), and it's got to contain one immensely long and immensely varied woman's part. Which is exactly, my dear boy, *exactly* what you've done. It's amazing."

For a moment longer Alistair held out against rapture. "But do you think she can do it?" he said. "After all, it's rather different from revue. . . ."

"Than which," observed his host, "there is no better training in the world. If Camilla takes it on you'll be safe for a year's run and royalties to match. Look here, if I rang her up this minute, we might just catch her between the acts. Shall I?"

"You—you know her, then?" asked Alistair feebly.

"*Know* her? Good God, boy, we've been sweethearts for years!" said Mr. Paget simply; and apparently taking Alistair's speechlessness for consent went over to the 'phone.

Weak with excitement, the fortunate dramatist could only cling to his chair and pray silently. There was a cold, uneasy feeling in the pit of his stomach, ready to develop into either exultation or biliousness as occasion should demand. In a sweat of nervousness he listened to Raymond Paget's mellow notes purling into the mouthpiece. . . .

"That you, Camilla darling? Raymond speaking. Raymond Paget. Listen, I've found you a play. Yes, marvellous. The best woman's part I've ever read, bar none. . . . An infant prodigy, I found him in the Park. . . . This afternoon. Right. We'll be there. Right. *Au revoir*, my dear."

He hung up the receiver with a triumphant click and turned back to his protégé.

"She wants us to go round after the show and talk it over . . . which means almost at once. I'll 'phone for a taxi. Because this, my son, is where things begin to move. Do you think you can put it across without another drink?"

"No," said Alistair firmly.

CHAPTER XIII

I

THE small, crowded dressing-room was not nearly so splendid as Alistair had expected, for his visits to the Komfy

Kinema had given him a very high standard of back-stage luxury; but as soon as Miss Dane entered all minor disappointments were swamped in a wash of personality. She was a really beautiful woman of twenty-five or forty, with large brown eyes, hair like burnished copper, and a genuinely dazzling smile. It travelled round the room like the beam of a searchlight, seeming to illumine not only her own countenance, but also that of her *vis-à-vis*, so that all present acquired a brilliant artificial glow; and observing this phenomenon Alistair was able to correct his first impression. It wasn't a searchlight, that smile, it was The Limes.

The next instant he received the beam full in the face and was left gasping.

"So this," said Miss Dane, "is our brilliant young man!"

Alistair grinned feebly, and was slapped on the back by Raymond Paget.

"An unknown genius," Mr. Paget assured her, "whom I found sitting on the steps of the Albert Memorial at half-past three this afternoon. Seriously, my dear, you're going to be very, very grateful to me. His play's got the best woman's part since Cinderella."

The great brown eyes widened greedily.

"Have you got it with you?"

"I'm afraid it—it's not entirely written yet," apologized Alistair, finding his voice for the first time. "But I've got the scenario." He produced his folder, and prayerfully offered her the slender typescript. But Miss Dane waved it aside.

"I can't take in anything unless I hear it read aloud. Just show me how the play begins and I'll tell you if I want to hear any more."

Now the first scene was one of the very best, and though literally trembling with excitement Alistair was by now sufficiently intoxicated to give it for all it was worth. Hardly referring to the script, he plunged into the frantic orgy of night-life on a revolving stage; cabarets, night-clubs, *boîtes*, restaurants, all whizzing round at top speed and to half a dozen different orchestras. Then the great whirligig slows down, and Jennifer Torch—that's Miss Dane—makes her first entrance. She is running down a great zigzag fire-escape (it is in one of the outdoor segments), while at innumerable windows gentlemen in evening dress lean out and grab at her. She kicks off all their hats.

From this spirited beginning she proceeds to all the other haunts of vice, where, for her coming, lights burn brighter, drums beat faster, champagne flows like water.

They press her to stay, until suddenly—boom! All is in darkness, while Big Ben strikes five.

"And then," said Alistair solemnly, "in the dim grey light of early dawn, the great wheel begins to turn again. But quite slowly, and quite silently, for all the revellers are gone. Only one shadowy figure returns, and she too is silent. It is Jennifer, walking in her sleep. She glides down the great fire-escape, and through the empty dance-halls. She is looking for something. She is looking for her wedding-ring."

He paused for breath, and found the great brown eyes gazing at him with something almost like awe.

"Christ!" said Miss Dane.

After a respectful interval the rest of the party joined in polyglot expressions of admiration and amazement, and thus reminded of their presence she turned, aloofly. "Please go away, every one. This is going to be important. And Maurice"—a swarthy young gentleman sprang to attention—"just see if Mr. Markham is by any chance still in the building. I saw him in the manager's room as we came by."

Like an arrow from the bow Maurice sped on his errand. Almost as swiftly the other gentlemen made their adieux. As soon the room was clear Miss Dane opened a private cupboard and produced a bottle of champagne.

"We'll drink to the Future," she said gloriously, "yours and mine. And Raymond here shall have a spoonful because he brought us together."

In the midst of these celebrations Mr. Markham made his appearance, and was immediately accommodated with a tooth-glass. He was a wiry little man with clipped grey hair and monkey eyes: and with the wisdom of experience he drank first and questioned after.

"My part," said Miss Dane simply. "He'd got it all the time, Jimmy, hidden in his pram." She indicated the now brazen dramatist and added a few words in explanation of Raymond Paget. "Honest, Jimmy, it's the greatest thing I've ever struck. Real drama, yet not highbrow. I tell you, it's the goods."

"I should like to hear it," said Mr. Markham.

Nothing loath, Alistair began once more at the beginning, and this time worked right through to the end. The balcony scene, the door-slamming, the temporary distraction, all made their points. Inspired by the champagne, fresh beauties sprang up under his labouring tongue—in the trial scene, for instance, Jennifer not only defended her husband on a charge of murder, but for the murder of his mistress; and when he finally reached the death-bed lip-stick Miss Dane exclaimed aloud.

"Jimmy," she ordered tempestuously, "say it's great. Say it's the greatest ever. Say you'll put it on for me as soon as we get rid of this God-awful song and dance." Her eyes, her teeth, her brazen hair—all blazed at him with sublime entreaty; but Mr. Markham kept his head.

"I should like first," he ruled, "to see the complete script. But it certainly seems to have possibilities."

"Possibilities!" She flung herself on Alistair like a protective tigress. "Don't take any notice of him, my dear, a hundred years ago he'd have crabbed Shakespeare. He knows it's the goods as well as I do, and he knows that when I want a thing it generally happens. Possibilities, indeed!"

Alistair poured himself out some more champagne. It steadied him wonderfully. Very calmly and courteously, though at a considerable distance, he heard himself say:

"Then do I understand that, the completed work being still what Miss Dane wants, you will undertake to produce the play?"

"If it's what *I* want," said Mr. Markham, "I'll put it on in March."

Miss Dane jumped up and kissed him on both cheeks. "You old devil!" she cried gayly. "Frightening me out of my life!" She kissed him again.

"You'd better not do that," said Mr. Markham. "I've got a slight cold. Now see here, young man, when can you let me have the finished thing?"

Alistair thought rapidly. He very much wanted to ask how long a play ought to be, but the question seemed unsuitable. Not more than fifty thousand words, surely, and if he wrote two thousand a day, it would be ready in a month. Add say a week for typing. . . .

"The end of next month," he said firmly.

"That ought to do. You might let me have that opening scene as soon as it's ready, though. I'll be interested to see how it works out."

"In a week's time," promised Alistair.

"Send me a copy too," begged Miss Dane. "Jimmy's so stingy he won't lend me his, he says I lose them; but he's a great little man all the same, and never says a word he doesn't mean." Jimmy sneezed. "Honest, Mr. French, you couldn't have had better luck in the world than running straight into Jimmy with your first play."

"Except," amended Alistair, "running into you." And as he gazed full into the limelight, he felt their two superior souls not only click but clinch.

"Write soon," said Miss Dane softly, and gave him her hand.

"I suppose you can leave this scenario with me now?" asked Mr. Markham, picking up the folder.

There being a carbon copy at home, Alistair agreed willingly.

"And now," sighed Camilla Dane, "I must be going along. I need as much sleep as a baby." With flattering reluctance she withdrew her hand and picked up a magnificent ermine cloak. Alistair wrapped it tenderly round her no less snowy shoulders. Raymond Paget found the embroidered bag. They all three escorted her downstairs to the waiting car, but it was Alistair whose hand assisted her at the turnings. She may even have kissed him at parting, but he could never quite remember.

When the big Rolls had moved away, Mr. Markham hailed a passing taxi and said briefly:

"Well, good-night, French. Let me hear from you as soon as possible. 'Night, Paget. Go another walk in the Park sometime, will you?"

The door banged to, and they stood alone on the steps of the theatre.

"Well," said Mr. Paget inadequately.

Alistair nodded.

"Come and have a drink," said Mr. Paget, sitting down abruptly on the top step.

But Alistair had a previous engagement. He was going to tell Cressida.

CHAPTER XIV

I

CONSIDERING the severe emotion under which he laboured, and his imperfect knowledge of the ground, it was small wonder if Alistair took longer than was strictly necessary to get from the Haymarket to Carey Street. He went on foot, because 'buses were by this time very scarce, and because it did not occur to him to take a cab. His speed, however, could not have been much under five miles an hour; and with the assistance of the police (many of whom he completely misunderstood), he reached Bloomsbury shortly before one in the morning.

About this point it struck him that he had forgotten the number of the house. As far as he could recollect, it was about next but one to the far end—assuming, of course, that he entered the street from his original direction; and these speculations occupied him so completely that he might have overshot the turning altogether but for a lucky collision at the required corner.

"Look where you're going, can't you?" snapped his victim.

Alistair did so, and saw a short, swarthy, remarkably broad-shouldered young gentleman in evening dress.

Time being precious, he apologized as insultingly as possible and hurried on.

Never in all his life had he seen houses that looked so much alike. They each had a strip of garden, a flight of steps, and a pointed porch. If it wasn't the one next to the end he would have to start ringing the bells. . . .

And then suddenly he saw her. She was standing under one of the porches, letting herself in with a latchkey: and just in time he called quickly:

"Cressida!"

She looked down and saw, standing under the lamp-post, brightly lit as a figure on the stage, a character actor in the part of Alistair French. Every line and movement of his upturned face was defined with dramatic clarity: the actor had ruffled his hair, blued his eyelids, stressed the romantic shadow under the cheekbone: he was the Alistair of Alistair's dreams. Then she looked again and saw that he was also Romeo at the balcony, de Bergerac before the Spanish lines, and Shakespeare's Henry the Fifth.

But under the shadow of the porch Alistair could see only the white oval of her face and the white fur about her throat: and to these he called, "Cressida!" meaning Helen, Lucrece, Iseult, Madonna.

"What is it?" she asked, the door half-closed behind her.

"Come down, Cressida. I've got something to tell you."

(To go up the steps, he was thinking, to go up the steps and be close to her in that sheltered darkness. To push aside the fur, and find her shoulder smooth and sweet-smelling and warm in the darkness. To push the warm fur from her sweet shoulder, to feel her smooth throat filling his hands, to follow with his hands the subtle curve from ear to sweet warm shoulder. . . .)

"Come down, Cressida," he cried again, holding fast by the railings. The door clicked shut behind her and she came out of the warm sweet shadow down the white steps. She must have been to the theatre, or dancing; she wore a long pale dress and a short furred coat of black velvet.

"Well?" she asked.

But Alistair could not tell her as quickly as that. Instead he swept his arm towards Orion and said:

"It's a lovely night. Come and walk."

"My dear, you must be mad!" (But she did not seem in the least alarmed, only wondering.) "It's after one."

"Not long after."

"And I shall ruin my shoes."

Alistair looked down at her silver slippers. She was quite right, they were too beautiful to spoil. In another moment he had pulled off his overcoat and was about to spread it on the pavement when Cressida seized his shoulder.

"My dear, you really are mad," she said resignedly. "I suppose that means I shall have to humour you. Put on your coat again, and we'll pick out the nice clean patches."

So picking out the nice clean patches they made their way down the road and presently came to a square with trees in it. They walked round it once, twice, and still Alistair had not found his tongue. It was so exquisite to be strolling beside his love in the frosty night that any words—even the words that strung together should tell of his fortune—seemed a jarring of perfection. But at last Cressida plucked at his sleeve and said sleepily: "Alistair . . . I want to go to bed."

In spite of her long dress she looked so like a tired child that he almost picked her up and carried her home. But first he had something to tell her, and all at once he was swept up on a great wave of elation.

"Listen," he said, "listen, Cressida, because it's happening to us, and it's frightfully exciting. Have you ever heard of an actress called Camilla Dane?"

In an instant the sleepy child had vanished. Miss Drury stared at him suspiciously.

"Camilla Dane? Of course I have. She's in revue."

"She won't be long," said Alistair. "Have you heard of a man called Markham?"

"He's her manager. But why?"

"Because as soon as this God-awful song and dance comes to an end Mr. Markham is going to star Camilla Dane in a play by me."

The effect was all he could have desired. Cressida stood perfectly still in the middle of the pavement. She was deprived of speech. Only her eyes adored him.

"Fixed it up just now, in Miss Dane's dressing-room," said Alistair carelessly, and wondering at the same time what she would do if he suddenly kissed her.

Her voice had returned, sweet with the honey of admiration, caressing as the touch of a lover's hand. She said:

"It's the most wonderful thing I've ever heard of. It—it's like a miracle. Alistair, do you know that you're the luckiest young man in the world?"

Alistair nodded. The fur at her throat had fallen apart, revealing a new and exquisite line from ear to chin. Before such beauty he felt his own success a thing too trivial to be spoken of. He wanted simply to look. But Cressida thought otherwise, and now asked him whether he had a definite contract.

"Nothing on paper, so far," said Alistair lightly, "but Markham's got the scenario."

"Then you ought to go round and see him in the morning. My dear, it's no good; in these days one simply has to be business-like. Try and get a definite agreement for production within the next six months, or at any rate within a year—"

Alistair listened, faintly impatient. The business side was very important, no doubt, and would eventually have to be attended to; but not now. Just now he wanted to give himself up to pure feeling.

"Let's walk," he said, as soon as she had stopped speaking; and with a quick upward glance of her grey eyes Cressida obeyed. She seemed to have lost her weariness, moving by his side with a beautiful slow swing that sent her pale skirts swishing against his ankle. The broad trimming of the jacket sleeves made a muff for her clasped hands, and Alistair thought how warm and snug they must be under the white fur. He wanted to touch it, and the velvet of her shoulder: but was prevented by the awful chivalry of callow love.

Half-way round the square they halted again, this time under a lamp, where he could see her more clearly.

"Do you realize," said Alistair, "that this is only the third time we've been together?"

"You should have come and seen me," said Cressida.

"I did—don't you remember? You were trying on a yellow hat."

"Of course! There were those dreadful women. . . . But you should have come again."

"I didn't think you wanted me."

"Of course I wanted you . . ."

Greatly daring, he reached out and took her by the shoulders. With a trustfulness that wrung his heart she stood quite still . . . waiting, no doubt, for him to speak.

"Be my friend always," he said. It was the nearest he could get to the tumult in his soul, but she seemed to understand.

He elaborated.

"You see . . . I know I'm going to be a success. I'm going to go all over the place and meet all sorts of people: but I've got to have something behind it." His grip on her shoulders tightened, drawing her towards him. "We're here together at the beginning, Cressida. Will you see it through with me?"

"Through to the end, my dear," she said steadily.

For a moment longer they stood in silence, swearing fellowship with their eyes. Then Alistair released her with a sigh.

"And now I suppose I must take you home," he said. Cressida sighed too, for her dramatic training had given her a horror of anti-climax.

"I suppose you must," she murmured. A more experienced ear might have detected a faint upward inflection, the inflection of doubt or inquiry. But not Alistair's.

II

There was a letter waiting for him when he got back, a letter from Uncle Severus. He inquired after his nephew's health, and reiterated the offer, should circumstances arise to make it acceptable, of a post with Clark and Bailey.

Twice in the night Alistair woke up laughing.

CHAPTER XV

I

SUNDAY is a day of rest, and both Henry and Alistair slept soundly till after eleven. Shortly after that hour there was a great stirring of blankets in the bed by the window, and Henry's tousled head came burrowing up to the light.

"Hello," he said. "Are you awake?"

But Alistair lay deceitfully still within his warm cocoon. In spite of a slight headache, his thoughts were so beautiful that he could not bear to leave them, even for the pleasure of hearing Henry marvel. Just at the moment he was engaged on a detailed reconstruction of the walk with Cressida. . . .

"Here, wake up," shouted Henry brutally. "It's your turn to make the coffee."

With exquisite reluctance Alistair withdrew his hands from her velvet shoulders and began to unwind himself. It was very cold outside, and his dressing-gown, instead of being at the foot of the bed, lay far away on the floor. Henry could reach it if he stretched.

"Chuck me my dressing-gown, will you?" said Alistair amiably. "Winter seems to be upon us."

"Anything else you'd like?" asked Henry, flinging the garment with unnecessary violence.

Alistair looked up in surprise. For some reason, it seemed, old Henry was annoyed with him. But why? They hadn't met since the previous afternoon, and he was all right then. Or—was it possible they *had* met at some subsequent point, which he had since forgotten in the rush of events? Now he came to think of it, he did vaguely remember seeing Henry's face quite late in the evening.

Suddenly it all came back. The mad hurry from the restaurant, the firelit room, himself bursting in and lighting the gas, Henry glaring furiously over a girl's head. . . .

Overcome by embarrassment he retreated once more beneath the bedclothes to think things over. It was obviously impossible to apologize, for that would look as though he had noticed; but on the other hand, some explanation was imperative. What, if anything, he had said at the time was now a matter for conjecture only; quite possibly in his excitement he had merely made bad worse. Alistair burrowed a little deeper, where it presently struck him that the only thing to do was to relate the whole miraculous story and leave Henry to draw his own conclusions. It would surely be obvious that a person who was just having his fortune made could hardly stop to cough at doors. . . .

"Time for lunch soon," said Henry with restraint.

Alistair leapt out of bed and stood on his hands. At any other time he would have been the first to condemn so childish a method of breaking the great news; but he now wanted to fix Henry's attention without delay. He succeeded.

"Are you still drunk?" said Henry coldly.

"I'll never be sober again," said Alistair, slowly waving his legs. Directly under his nose lay the letter from Uncle Severus, and the sight of it made him laugh so much that he had to come down.

Henry, who was by this time looking at him with real alarm, stooped and picked it up. The case seemed serious, and Alistair obviously out of his wits. He read the letter through.

"I don't see anything so funny about that," he said.

"It isn't. It's the context." And still fighting for breath, Alistair led him step by step through all the events of the previous day, beginning at the Albert Memorial and ending under the portico of the Majestic Theatre. (The last perfect chapter he eliminated entirely, not on account of its intimacy—to the artist nothing is sacred—but realizing that in some eyes it might even be considered an anti-climax. Or so he told himself. In any case, the tale was quite long enough already.)

Henry followed, goggling. Breakfast was forgotten; without thinking about it they had both got back into bed. As soon as Alistair had finished he went back to the beginning and took the whole thing through again, but this time more slowly, so that the audience could ask questions. The personal appearance of Mr. Paget was discussed in great detail, until Henry had a perfect recollection of seeing him at the Embryo. He also remembered, after very little coaching, having applauded Camilla Dane in a musical comedy, and listened with eagerness to the reported conversation of Mr. Markham. By the time they had rehearsed it all for the third time it was nearly one o'clock.

"Never mind," said Alistair recklessly. "We'll go and have a blow-out at the Riviera. I could eat a house."

Henry thrust one foot out of bed and paused.

"What about all this crowd? Are you going to tell them?"

Alistair too checked, half-way into his trousers.

"No," he decided, "not yet. They all want such a frightful lot of explanation, especially Mr. Hickey. I suppose it comes of having to do with machinery. But I tell you what I *will* do, I'll have 'em all to the first night."

II

But he nearly changed his mind when they entered the café and found all their friends neatly assembled at the various tables. There was Winnie and Charlie and Eddie Cribb, Mrs. Griffin (a rare visitor, this, since she was generally fed by her ladies), Arnold Comstock reading a book, and finally, toying majestic with his private beer, Mr. Hickey himself. They were all sitting in silence, as though waiting for some important announcement, and Alistair's resolution was at cracking-point when Winnie suddenly banged the table with her knife and cried:

"Oh, come on! What's the odds so long as you're happy?"

He then perceived that what they had taken for vacuum had been merely a lull in some violent argument; and as the smouldering flames once more leapt up he began to get the hang of it. It had all been started, it seemed, by Winnie Parker.

This did not surprise him in the least, for with the approach of Christmas Winnie's spirits, never low, had risen to an unexampled pitch of hilarity. Her convictions were less religious than social: she liked every one to enjoy themselves on the proper occasions, and personally intended to enjoy herself very much indeed. Charlie and some of the boys were taking her to the Panto, Eddie's Club had another Gala, and there was a Hundred Per Cent. Jollity Dance at the local hall. But she had also another project, even more to her taste, which was that Number Fifteen should give a Christmas party; and this she had now been putting before the public for the first time. The public, however, were not enthusiastic. They said they would turn it over in their minds: and this was what they had been doing when Henry and Alistair came in.

"You'll find it an awful lot of work," prophesied Charlie Coe.

"I don't care, I'll do it," said Winnie recklessly. Her blue eyes swept over them in a fury of impatience. Sitting there like a lot of sacks!

"If you must have any more excitement," proceeded Charlie, "what about all going and having dinner at one of the Corner Houses? That's worth the money, that is, and it's all the same thing."

"'Course it isn't. For one thing, Ma wouldn't see it, and I want her to have a bit of fun. Look, we'd all make lists of who we want to ask"—she leant half across the table, hypnotizing them into gayety—"and I'll write the invitations, I'll do everything. There'll have to be paper chains, o' course, and perhaps some of the boys'll lend a hand with those, but that's all. Just you write your list and leave the rest to Winnie. I've got mine here now."

"Let's see." Charlie took the piece of paper from her and flattened it among the breadcrumbs.

"Where d'you think of 'aving it?" asked Mrs. Griffin suspiciously. "All our rooms are as narrer as coffins."

"Not Mr. Hickey's isn't." Winnie turned eagerly to the gentleman in question, who happened to be sitting at the next tables and put her arm round his neck. "You'd let us use it, wouldn't you? We'd be ever so careful and clean it all up afterwards, truly we would. Go on, Mr. Hickey, there's an old love!"

Under this sudden attack Mr. Hickey's powers of speech, always laggard, appeared to forsake him altogether; but it was noticed (and afterwards much deplored) that he made no attempt to free himself.

"See here, Win, don't you know *any* girls?" asked Charlie, looking up from the piece of paper. "You've got 'leven names here, all fellows. . . ."

"'Leven? I made it twelve," said Winnie nonchalantly. "Anyway, they're nearly all your friends, I thought you'd like to have them."

"Yes, but you ought to have some girls. It—it's only proper."

"So I have. I've got Nina."

Charlie looked up cautiously.

"She'll be here still, I s'pose?"

"'Course she will. She's looking forward to it ever so."

"I see 'er go off just now looking ever so smart," said Mrs. Griffin meaningly. Neither she nor any one else knew what the meaning was, but as a manner of speech it lent weight to her conversation.

"That's right. She's gone to the pictures with Sid Mason. Reg gave us a whole lot of tickets." She caught Charlie's eye and directed it towards Mr. Cribb. "Aren't you jealous, Ed?"

The boxer shook his head and went on eating. They were always telling him things about this girl Nina, and he couldn't for the life of him see why. A washed-out looking piece, with eyes that rolled about like a doll's. . . .

"Even if you have got Nina that's only two," said Charlie, returning doggedly to the point. "There ought to be more than that."

"Well, why don't you bring some yourself? I don't care, I'm going to dance with Mr. Hickey."

"Dance?" echoed Mrs. Griffin. She was not really a kill-joy, but she felt she ought to have been consulted earlier.

"O' course. One of the boys has got a jazz band, and he's going to borrow a gramophone as well, and Charlie can bring his uke."

"Thank you," said Charlie, with some sarcasm. "That's very kind of you. I made sure you wouldn't be wanting me, what with the jazz band and all."

"Now, now!" said Mr. Hickey surprisingly. "No unpleas-antness. If I'm going to let you have my room— mind, I don't say I am, but if I do—I don't want no squabbling." He paused, and his majestic eye—the eye that from the eminence of the driver's seat looked down even upon policemen—travelled slowly over the company. "Now, what about drinks?"

"Beer," said Charlie Coe promptly.

"And port wine for the ladies."

In awed silence they watched him extract a pencil and write it down. There was a general feeling that if once Mr. Hickey took the thing up it was bound to be a success.

"Now, how many are there likely to be? You say you got eleven there?"

"That's right," said Charlie. "All fellows."

"Counting yourself?"

"No. Twelve with me. If I come, that is."

"Say, two dozen bitter," wrote Mr. Hickey. "Now, what about you, Mr. French? I hope we're to have the pleasure of your company?"

"I say, that's awfully decent of you," said Alistair, who for some minutes had been experiencing all the emotions of the child waiting to be asked.

"Not at all," replied the 'bus-driver graciously, "and your friend, too, if he cares to come. Say, two bottles 'Black and White'."

"Not for me, I hope," interposed Alistair hastily.

"No? You going to drink beer with the youngsters? Very well, then, say two and a half dozen in case of emergencies. We'll leave the whisky at two, because I might bring along a pal from the Depôt myself. Now, as to food—"

"The ladies'll see to that," cried Winnie. "I can make jellies something lovely."

"Here, you going to drink port?" asked Charlie, looking over Mr. Hickey's shoulder.

"Not me. I'm a T.T. But it'll make Ma's eyes shine all right."

"I'll bring a bottle of lemon squash. See here, Win, if you're going to have dancing you got to get some more girls. 'Sfar as I can see," said Charlie, "ther'll be twelve fellows without partners."

Winnie licked her spoon resourcefully.

"Tell 'em to bring their sisters."

"Chaps don't want to dance with their sisters."

"Oh, get back into the oven," said Winnie, "you're half-baked." And heedless of his angry looks she resumed her flirtation with Mr. Hickey.

III

"I say, are you really a teetotaler?" asked Alistair a little later, as he and Winnie walked back down Bloom Street. It seemed an odd trait in one so frankly appreciative of, so admirably fitted to appreciate, the transitory pleasures.

"You bet I am," said she; "you ought to have seen my old Dad," She quickened her step to a kind of heel-and-toe patter dance, jumping in and out of the gutter like a puppy on a string. "Isn't Mr. Hickey a wonder? I never would have believed it, honest I wouldn't. I'm going to kiss him under the mistletoe."

"And Charlie, too, I hope," said Alistair. It seemed to him a good moment to put in a tactful word for that hardly used young man. "He's a nice lad, young Charlie, and pretty good at his job. I know he puts up with a deuce of a lot, but one day he may get tired of it; and if you aren't careful—"

"And if *you* aren't careful," said Winnie tersely, "you'll get your head smacked." With which timely warning she disappeared up the path.

CHAPTER XVI

I

BUT . . .

"Quietly, *please*, Alistair," said Aunt Gertrude.

For after all he had not been destined to partake of Mr. Hickey's "Black and White." Like Henry, he returned to Norbury for the festive season and spent seven days gloomily overeating at Stanley Avenue.

He had gone simply because he could think of no excuse for staying away, and bitterly regretted the gayeties of Number Fifteen. Aunt Gertrude was even more trying than usual, having developed, as though in mourning for her late brother-in-law, an extreme sensitiveness to all forms of sound. The banging of a door, the abrupt closing of a book even, was sufficient to upset her nerves for an entire evening; and side by side with this infirmity had sprouted an equally strong dislike of being left alone. Her usual companion, an indigent second cousin, had escaped into the provinces for the period of Alistair's visit, and he was therefore completely without support. Their only visitor was Uncle Severus, who turned up on Boxing Day, cocked an inquiring eye, and took his nephew for a long walk. No reference, however, was made to the firm of Clark and Bailey, nor did Alistair allude to his own approaching fame. It was not so much modesty as a prescient weariness of spirit: he did not want to have to explain to Aunt Gertrude, for instance, why it was quite all right for him to have gone home with what was practically a strange man. She would know everything in due course—probably through the medium of a box for the first night—but in the meantime he kept his own counsel.

Henry too was sworn to silence. The friends met only once during this period, after church on Christmas morning, and bore the separation without much pain; each being, in fact, secretly glad of a rest from the other's company. (Mrs. Brough and Aunt Gertrude, who did not understand this, were constantly urging them to bring one another in to tea: but they prevaricated with equal success.) Apart from the gradually decreasing richness of the food all seven days were very much alike. Alistair had brought his typewriter home with him, and by taking a card-table into the bathroom succeeded in dodging both Aunt Gertrude's nerves and Aunt Gertrude's curiosity. Here, in overcoat and muffler, he actually completed and typed out the first scene of his masterpiece (which was now called *Luna Park*), and also wrote a long covering letter to Mr. Markham pointing out its various beauties. The rest of the time had to be spent in the drawing-room with his aunt, where he sat for hours on end thinking about Cressida and doing the crosswords out of the morning land evening papers. On New Year's Eve they sat up religiously until midnight, when Alistair, being suitably dark, went out of the front door into a slight drizzle, and performed the ritual of first-footing.

The next day he went back to Bloom Street, where he found Number Fifteen just recovering from a perfect orgy of good-will. Paper chains festooned the hall, broken meats proclaimed the recent abundance, and Winnie had received no fewer than eighteen Christmas presents, mostly from gentlemen.

"How did the party go off?" asked Alistair wistfully.

"Something lovely! Why, we didn't get them out of the house till three in the morning. Mr. Hickey had a friend what recited, pretending to be a little nipper, like, and we nearly died laughing. It was a shame you couldn't hear him."

"I wish I had," said Alistair in a markedly low voice. They were walking along Kimberly Street at the time, and many passers-by showed a natural interest. But the hint had no effect.

"And as for Ma," shrilled Winnie, "she was fair blotto from the word go. Because o' course she got to the port right at the beginning, and after that there was no holding her. She chased Mr. Hickey all round the room with a bit of mistletoe. She *did* have a good time."

"And what about Mr. Hickey?"

"Well, if you ask me," said Winnie frankly, "I'd say he'd had one over the eight himself. The things he said to Nina you wouldn't believe! I got ever so worried, knowing how refined she is, but the boys said it didn't mean nothing, not after all that whisky."

For some minutes they walked on in silence, meditating on the idiosyncrasies of the great, until the traffic from a side-street stopped them on the curb. Immediately opposite was a barrow stacked with yellow narcissus, pale pink tulips, branches of mimosa, marigolds, sturdy jonquils, and the first bright daffodils.

"Coo, aren't they early?" cried Winnie.

Alistair nodded.

"Earlier than they used to be. 'Daffodils,'" he quoted softly, "'that come before the swallow dares, and take the winds of March with beauty.'"

"What things you do think of!" said Winnie admiringly.

II

The year slipped by with deceitful swiftness. They took down the paper chains, bought a bunch of tulips, and it was spring. Henry went home for the Easter vacation and returned almost at once. In his little room at the Majestic Mr. Markham read the first scene of *Luna Park* and subsequently dictated a letter. Winnie at last succeeded in finding Nina a job, not of course on the stage, but in a shop similar to her own and even more conveniently situated. And in the room on the top floor Alistair sat doing his accounts and thinking about Cressida.

He never seemed to get any farther with her.

The conversation under the lamp-post had brought them at one stride to a degree of intimacy which made all other relations seem thin and colourless: but after four months the friendship thus begun had become less a miracle than a habit. They met constantly, Alistair calling daily at Carey Street between the hours of five and six. Quite often she was out, but even so they could never have seen each other less than four or five times a week. (It often amused Alistair to think that of all these meetings and emotions, of all this wonder and romance, running parallel to his own humdrum life, old Henry knew absolutely nothing. If any one had asked him how to get hold of Cressida Drury he would have replied, doubtfully, "Blessed if I know. Why don't you try Pooh?" Whereas Alistair—and this made the situation even more piquant—knew absolutely everything about old Henry. In the morning he set off for his Training College, in the evening he either went out with other members thereof or worked at home; and that was all.) On one or two occasions Cressida came to the house at Bloom Street (always, of course, when Henry was out), but Alistair was too nervous to enjoy her presence there to the full. He was afraid of old Ma Parker, and of the unseemly comment that would inevitably follow an encounter on the stairs.

"You've no idea how awful she is," he told Cressida feelingly. It was a rash thing to say, for Cressida naturally demanded chapter and verse, and even threatened to pay a formal visit to the Parker *ménage*. She had seen Winnie in the hall and thought her delightful.

"So she is," agreed Alistair, with a grin of recollection for Winnie's upturned face gaping through the banisters. Admiration had never been more frank. "She thinks you're ever so distinguished."

Cressida had laughed, not ill-pleased. She was as eager for praise as a cat for cream, and Alistair, with a lover's instinct, almost unconsciously took advantage of this trait to make himself more and more necessary to her. It was scarcely vanity: vanity was too frivolous for the deep, almost solemn admiration with which Cressida regarded her own person. Her attitude was extreme, but not unreasonable; she did not exaggerate, she merely appreciated; and, adoring beauty, necessarily adored herself. Nor was she without a touch of altruism which, mingling with this other strain, produced curious results. She knew it gave people pleasure to see her, and definitely resented the waste of beauty that flowed unremarked in her least action. She liked to be watched, and when Alistair came to her room in the evenings would immediately begin performing a dozen minor duties which could easily have been done earlier in the day. Flowers were arranged, cushions shaken, a packet of cigarettes emptied into the Chinese box, while he sat on the edge of the bed and followed her movements with adoring eyes. Once he said: "When you're here alone—do you ever do anything?" She looked at him unsmiling.

"Yes. I learn parts."

And that was the other Cressida, the fiercely ambitious actress-adventurer who had said she would die if she had not achieved success at twenty-five. To arrive at this end she was prepared to work with cold fury: she would be, eventually, the star who was never late for a rehearsal; and more even than the straitening of her means did she resent, in the state of resting, its forced inactivity.

So after mornings spent at the agents Cressida came back and sat down to learn the parts of Juliet, Millamant, Peter Pan, Cleopatra, Paula Tanqueray, Saint Joan, La Dame aux Camelias, Hedda Gabler. Sometimes she would make Alistair take the book and play whole scenes with her, returning time after time to an intonation, a gesture, a silence, with which she was not quite satisfied. He was not much of a help to her, being far deeper in love than is good for the judgment; but he did his best, and incidentally added considerably to his knowledge of English literature.

But still he got no farther. There was nothing tangible, nothing definite of which he could say: This is what stops me. But there are some atmospheres so diamond-clear that in them things distant seem close at hand; and through such deceiving air did Cressida move. She would call him My dear, angel, Alistair darling: lean on his shoulder to reach a cigarette: and never lose her cool remoteness. Once, in the very early days, he had tried to speak of love and devotion, but hardly reached to the end of a sentence. She did not chide or snub him, she merely withdrew—as she withdrew from all emotion, unless simulated. There was nothing aloof in her playing of Cleopatra, no crystal coldness in her Juliet. She kept her passions, it seemed, in their proper place—the prompt-book.

So Alistair too grew formal, shy of speaking about himself, obedient to her unspoken command. And he never showed her the play of Jennifer Torch.

Ever since the disaster of his second visit the script had continued to lie on his desk, waiting to be laid at the feet of the goddess. But even after Camilla Dane's rapturous approval, even after Cressida's own urgent demands, he could not bring himself to show it her: for he knew there was no love strong enough to blind her judgment of a play. Once, indeed, he carried the thing as far as Carey Street, only to lose heart at the last moment and conceal it under his hat. It was another matter in which he got no farther.

Away in Kimberly Street St. Peter's clock chimed for midnight. Alistair pushed back his chair and began to walk violently about the room.

The root of the trouble was not far to seek. His wooing lacked impressiveness. He should have been able to impose his will on hers from the very beginning, to sweep her off her feet and into his arms; but he was tied hand and foot in the strings of circumstance. Out of the kindness of her heart Cressida let him come and sit daily in her room: but a man should not say, "May I come in?", he should say, "Come out with me!" Alistair halted by the mantelpiece and stared bitterly at his face in the glass. No wonder she was kind, when his eyes implored pity like a sick dog's. Once she had stood bereft of speech in the middle of the pavement, and all from pure admiration; but that was a time they had both forgotten.

"My God, there must be something I can do," thought Alistair; and since it was not for the first time, the answer presented itself readily enough.

He ought, in the first place, to finish his play within the next fortnight: and in the second, to take her out much more frequently than heretofore.

For the whole trouble, of course, was that he was not writing a thousand words a day, nor anything like it. The comedy he was originally working on had been put aside in the interests of Jennifer Torch; but since the receipt of Mr. Markham's letter that too had somehow come to a standstill. The manager had returned the first scene *en bloc*, pointing out one or two of the more obvious defects, and suggesting that Alistair should study the work of certain well-known dramatists. For a week Alistair did so, becoming almost as assiduous as Mr. Puncher at the tables of the Free Library; an experiment which proved considerably more beneficial to his conversation than to his output.

Most of his time, indeed, was spent quite simply in thinking about Cressida, though he often passed whole hours at a time seated before the writing-table. He could think about hear there as well as anywhere, and after a morning in this position it was only common sense to go for a walk in the Gardens. Here, in pastoral musings, the hours slipped easily by until half-past three, when it was time to set out for Carey Street and the inexpressible pleasure of seeing her for the first time that day. It was, in its way, almost an ideal existence. But it did not provide for dinners at the Savoy.

Which brought him quite naturally to the question of accounts.

It will be remembered that these had never, in the early days, given him the least trouble. Rent, service, food, and fuel all added up to the sum of £1 10s. 2d., and indeed continued to do so; but on the current leaf of his note-book there appeared a new item for which he had made no provision. It ran, quite simply:

Cressida . . . . . 12s. 6d.

As the total outlay on two dinners, two teas, and a bunch of violets, the figure could hardly be considered other than extremely moderate; but it was enough, as an isolated extravagance, to unbalance Alistair's budget for the next month. And if, instead of being isolated, the extravagance was one of a progressive series, then was the outlook dubious indeed.

Staring down at the accusing figures Alistair realized for the first time the truth of the old tag about Racine. All Racine's heroes (as he, Alistair, had frequently pointed out to the Lower Fifth) were situated far above the cares of common life. Kings, emperors, victorious generals, they could dine their mistresses nightly without the slightest inconvenience. Hypolitus, for instance, passing a florist's window in Bond Street, could step in and order Aricie three dozen tea-roses without a second thought: and with what rapture, what kindliness, would Aricie receive them! For there was no doubt about it, women liked to be given things, and Cressida, three-parts angel as she was, could not entirely conceal her preference for decent meals.

Alistair closed his note-book and replaced it in his pocket. It was essential, he reasoned, that he should see her at least four times a week. She was his inspiration, his driving-force, his work demanded it; when you came to consider it coolly, in fact, four times was scarcely enough. This was obvious and needed no further discussion.

But . . .

Cressida . . . . . 12s. 6d.

Which made it equally obvious that another week or so at the present rate would see his finances thoroughly disorganized.

"Damn," said Alistair.

There was, of course, the possibility of dipping into his shallow capital, but the blood of highly solvent Presbyterians ran strong in his veins, and he was haunted in addition by the fear of having to appeal to Uncle Severus before his year was out.

"Damn," said Alistair again; and might have proceeded to even stronger expressions had he not been distracted by an urgent rapping at the door.

"Come in!" he substituted furiously.

It was Winnie, wearing a new black hat with a scarlet quill, so that for a moment he assumed, disgustedly, that she had called merely for admiration. But he was wrong.

"You going to be tramping up and down *all* night?" inquired Winnie politely.

CHAPTER XVII

I

ALISTAIR said rather curtly he was awfully sorry, but hadn't known he was annoying any one.

"Well, you are," said Winnie. "You're annoying Ma." Her sharp blue eyes slid round to the writing-table with its heaped papers and other signs of distress: but for once failed to soften. "When first we heard there was a writing-gentleman coming Ma said: 'Well, now we *shall* have some peace,' because the last gentleman played the uke in a cinema, and that naturally was a bit disturbing; but at least," finished Winnie, "something you liked to hear."

Alistair regarded her with surprise. It was the first time he had seen her in a mood even approaching anger: and the effect was startling. Her round eyes fairly blazed with annoyance, her whole body was vibrant with the fury of a very thin alley-cat defending its young; and Alistair, though otherwise completely at a loss, realized that only the most abject of apologies would have any effect.

"Look here," he said, "I really am most awfully sorry. I'd quite forgotten your grandmother would be in bed, or I'd have sat here like a statue and put my feet on the table—"

"Go on," said Winnie. "Laugh."

"Really, Winnie—"

But she could not explain. She knew only that he had offended against the one and only tenet of her faith—that of consideration for others. For Winnie's every act, through all the rough-and-tumble of daily circumstance, was informed with the most scrupulous regard for the sensibilities of her neighbours. She might chip Ma Parker, ride roughshod over the boys, and lead Charlie by the nose, but she had never in her life said an unkind word to any one of them. Her handling of impecunious youth was a model of delicacy—in the company of penniless admirers she invariably elected to eat at a coffee-stall, thus steering them safely between the extravagance of the Riviera and the humiliation of letting her pay for herself. The deepest emotion in her life, moreover, was her feeling for Ma Parker, a feeling purely maternal in depth and tenderness; and she had come in to find the old woman lying fretful and sleepless while overhead the impatient footfall of a literary gent shook the whole ceiling.

To Alistair her fury seemed entirely disproportionate. It was all very right and proper for Winnie to be fond of her objectionable relative, but there was no need to glare at him as though he had been trying to murder the old lady. With an air of considerable dignity, therefore, he repeated his apology and turned back to the desk.

"I can assure you," he added coldly, "that your grand-mother won't be disturbed again. And now, if you don't mind, there are several things I have to see to." He took up a random sheet of paper and scanned it importantly. "Cressida," it said, "12s. 6d."

But for some reason Winnie now showed no disposition to be gone. Her anger had burnt itself out, the nuisance had ceased, and for the first time she noticed that young Mr. French was looking ever so sad.

"Where's Mr. Brough?" she asked. 'I sh'd think you'd get bugs, always up here by yourself."

"This happens to be the first night I've been in this week," said Alistair, idiotically wounded.

"Oh!" Winnie looked at him doubtfully. He obviously didn't want her much, but on the other hand it was almost physically impossible for her to leave any suffering person. "Why don't you go to bed?" she ventured at last. "You look ever so tired . . ."

"I'm waiting for Cressida," said Alistair; and the next moment could have bitten his tongue out.

For perhaps ten seconds they stared at each other in silence. Then:

"I meant to say Henry," he added lamely.

There was no need to explain. Winnie might never have studied psychology, but she knew what was up when a boy who meant to say Henry said Cressida instead.

"That's your young lady, isn't it?" she asked gently. "The one I saw on the stairs?"

Alistair nodded.

"She's ever so beautiful."

Again Alistair nodded. All his early training bade him put an end to the conversation and show her politely downstairs; but on the other hand the longing to open his heart was like a physical distress. He yearned, he thirsted, to talk about Cressida. . . .

"Is she treating you bad?" asked Winnie sympathetically.

The simplicity of her approach was so disarming that instead of freezing her at once he replied, with equal straightforwardness:

"No. She's very kind to me. But somehow I can't—I can't get near her. And I never seem to—see her in the right sort of way. And even when she does come, I'm never sure she really wants to."

With extreme delicacy Winnie came to the point.

"I suppose she's used to being taken out in style?"

"That's it," agreed Alistair. He spoke without the slightest hesitation, but at the same time it struck him forcibly that he had no idea who took her. That miraculous evening before Christmas, for instance—she had evidently just come in from dancing; and now he often found her pale and languid after a late night. She never gave him any details.

"Perhaps you don't ask her often enough," said Winnie wisely.

Alistair shrugged.

"I can hardly keep asking her to come for a nice long walk. My God, I wish I were a millionaire!"

"Then you *would* be in a mess," quoth Winnie, "you'd have 'em all running you for your money. Besides, if she doesn't like walking, what's the matter with the pictures? You just say the word to Reggie Bennett and he'll get you as many seats as you like. He's ever such a nice boy."

"You don't understand," said Alistair ungratefully. Somehow or other they had got on to the wrong plane. "It's not just a question of theatre tickets. In any case, I'm not worth five minutes of her time."

"Oh, get back into the oven," said Winne. "What's it matter what you're worth, so long as she's fond of you?"

"Yes, but how can I *tell*?" demanded the furious lover. "That's what I want to know—how can I *tell*?"

"My goodness, d'you mean to say you haven't *asked* her?" countered Winnie.

They paused for breath. The conversation seemed to have reverted to its original key of fierce antagonism. Then Alistair said sulkily:

"Not in so many words."

This time it was Winnie's turn to shrug sarcastically.

"If that isn't just like a man!" she commented. "What about *her*, doesn't she want to know about you? You're all alike, you'll never speak till you're sure of the answer. Poor thing, I bet she'd give something to know if you was really serious."

"Serious!" groaned Alistair.

"Well, yes. It's ever so hard for a girl, you wouldn't believe. And often, like as not, some boy's let her down when she was quite a kid, and it's made her cautious. Why, look at me," said Winnie earnestly, "more'n a year ago, when I was just seventeen, I was going round with a boy from the chemist's. Ever so refined he was, and went to the L.C.C. classes every week. I used to wait for him outside—me I—and we'd walk about the streets for hours, him talking nineteen to the dozen. I thought it was wonderful. And then I met another boy who came from the same place—Salford, it was—and he told me Jim had been engaged to a girl there for the last year. Properly engaged, you know, with a ring." She paused, and sniffed rather violently. "Well, he'd never said nothing definite, so I suppose I hadn't nothing to complain of, but it took the curl out of me you wouldn't believe."

Alistair made vague commiserating noises.

"Oh, well, that's all over now," said Winnie philosophically. "But I've never slopped over on a boy since, and I've never waited outside the L.C.C. And perhaps that's how *she* feels."

In his sympathetic interest Alistair had quite lost sight of any personal application, and it was now with a slight sense of shock that he found himself required to draw a parallel between Cressida and the seventeen-year-old Winnie. For surely Cressida had never been so treated? Surely any man at whom she had so much as smiled would live and die her servant? . . . Yet Winnie was shrewd, and possibly knew more about feminine psychology than he did. It was quite true that he never had said anything—well, "definite": there had been no need when his every action was an implicit avowal; but so too, no doubt; were the actions of the faithless Jim. . . .

Winnie yawned.

"Well, I can't stay here all night," she observed practically. "I got to be up by seven. But you just sleep on what I've said, and see if I aren't right."

"It's been awfully decent of you to take so much trouble;" said Alistair sincerely. He got up to open the door, an attention which always gave her great pleasure, and would also have lit the landing gas had she not hastily protested against the waste of matches.

"I can see in the dark same as a cat;" she assured him. "Ma's got the door open, anyway. Get to bed before morning, won't you?"

Considerably touched by her solicitude, he promised to go almost at once; and having seen her safely downstairs returned to the table and began clearing up his papers. But he made a slow job of it, constantly falling into a reverie between one sheet and the next: and the upshot of his reflections was that proverbs can be very misleading. Actions might speak louder than words, but never half so plainly.

If Winnie were right—and he had already admitted her shrewdness and her inside information—then Cressida's lack of warmth was but the natural reserve of circumspect maidenhood. (Here a second proverb came into his head, the proverb of "Once bitten, twice shy"; but its crudeness repelled him.) In that case, all uncertainty could at once be ended by means of a formal declaration, after which he would automatically find his level as either the luckiest man in the world or an inhabitant of outer darkness.

He disliked the idea of outer darkness immensely.

And yet—at their last meeting, had she not called him "darling" twice in the space of an hour? *"But darling,"* (he remembered the exact words) *"I've got to be out by seven"*; and then just as he was leaving, *"Darling, do shut the window."* Surely that was more than just a manner of speech? He himself who in his private thought coupled her with Thaïs and Diana, had never ventured on the least endearment; but then women were notoriously less self-conscious.

Alistair thrust a sheaf of papers into the wrong drawer and tried to divorce the question from all personal feeling. But the feat was beyond his youthful powers; he knew only that he loved Cressida more than life, that she was drifting daily farther and farther away, and that the only way to hold her might equally well be the way to lose her forever.

It was a problem too great for any midnight solution, and remembering his promise to Winnie he had just decided to go to bed when Henry came in and began making tea.

II

This was so unusual a procedure for one of his Spartan temperament that Alistair stopped undressing to watch.

"Have a cup?" said Henry benevolently.

Surprised but grateful, Alistair accepted. After so much varied emotion the refreshment was extremely welcome; so instead of getting into bed he slipped on his dressing-gown and came back to the hearth. Henry was squatted on the rug waiting for the kettle, and either from proximity to the fire, or else from more subtle causes, his honest countenance was suffused with a crimson glow. Another interesting point was that his cropped fair hair seemed to have grown perceptibly since the morning.

"You look rather bucked about something," said Alistair at last.

As far as it was possible the glow deepened.

"I am," said Henry.

Alistair looked suitably excited.

"As a matter of fact," said Henry, "I—I've just got engaged."

Alistair's first emotion was one of plain annoyance. Having just decided to become engaged himself (for such is the power of emulation), he felt it rather unnecessary of Henry to have got in first in this underhand manner. But the conventions prevailed, and he offered his congratulation with appropriate heartiness.

"Thanks awfully, old man," said Henry, in a voice fairly slopping over with matyness. "I wanted you to be the first to know. It's Pamela, of course."

"Pamela?" repeated Alistair, interested but at a loss. "The one they call Eeyore. It's funny, but somehow, now we're engaged, I don't much care for it."

His friend nodded understanding. It was not a name to mingle smoothly in the raptures of passion.

"Pooh and Christopher Robin," continued Henry "have both got posts in a school at Bath. They're very pleased about it." He seemed to be catching at the skirts of a wider topic, but unable to obtain a hold.

"And what about Pamela?" asked Alistair helpfully.

"Well, it all depends. You see, I've just applied myself for a school at Willesden, and if I get it—it's quite a good screw—we might—we might," said old Henry, "get married next autumn."

The kettle boiled over.

CHAPTER XVIII

I

THE congratulations of Number Fifteen were hearty but absent-minded, for like Alistair's escape from death the news of Henry's engagement had clashed with another event of even greater significance. This was no less than Eddie Cribb's debut as a professional boxer, due to take place the following Friday at the hall in Handel Street, and until that was over no one had either thought or conversation for anything else.

The party from Bloom Street, as organized by Charlie Coe, was to consist of himself, Mr. Hickey, Reg Bennett, Henry and Alistair, and three other boys from Eddie's Club. Somewhat to Alistair's surprise Winnie, who did not usually hold back from a junketing, elected to stay at home, alleging that she could not abide the sight of blood; and though genuinely appreciative of her company no one pretended any disappointment that it was to be a stag party. To mark the importance of the occasion they were going in reserved seats.

"I'll nip along and get them tomorrow," decided Charlie, in his capacity of M.C. "I can easy do it after work, and then we shan't have to bother about being early."

At which point Winnie, looking up from her soup (for it was dinner-time at the Riviera), said casually:

"Don't forget Nina, will you?"

For a moment Charlie stared in silent dismay, spoon half-way to mouth and rendered speechless by the depth of his emotion.

"Nina?"

"That's right. She's coming."

"Not if I know it," said Charlie.

After which unprecedented display of insubordination he continued the upward movement of his spoon and took a mouthful of mulligatawny.

From the margin of her rouge to the roots of her hair Winnie's cheeks crimsoned with fury. Her eyes flashed, her lips trembled on the verge of repartee. Charlie continued to drink his soup. She drummed angrily on the cloth, still with no result; then, as the gravity of the situation began to dawn on her, she lowered the flag of battle and slipped round to the other side of the table.

"Come on, Charlie, be a sport," she urged, squeezing herself affectionately against the rebel's shoulder. "She wants to come ever so."

"Why?" said Charlie.

"'Cause she's sweet on Eddie Cribb, that's why. You know as well as I do."

"Then you can tell her from me it's a waste of time, because she gives Eddie a pain in the neck." He broke off and looked at her suspiciously, withdrawing a little in order to do so. "And see here, Win, don't you go putting ideas into people's heads. Eddie, he doesn't want no one sweet on him till he gives the word, and I won't be a party to it."

"Here, you want to finish this soup?" cried Clara the waitress, pausing by the plate on the other side of the table. "It'll be stone-cold in a minute."

More to conceal a slight embarrassment than because she really wanted it, Winnie reached across for her mulligatawny and also took the opportunity of ordering roast pork. It was funny how anything about Nina always seemed to get Charlie's goat. She gave him a few minutes to cool down and then tried again.

"I should have thought you'd have liked to be seen out with her, she always looks ever so smart. Sid Mason says she ought to be in the movies."

Charlie sniffed.

"Not that he's much to write home about," added Winnie hastily, feeling that she had been a little unfortunate in her authority; "but there's others as well. She's always being followed home."

Without deigning to comment he relinquished his soup-plate and turned to the menu. Winnie looked appealingly at Alistair, and Alistair looked at his pudding. But she was not yet defeated. To gain her end she would stick at nothing, not even surrender.

"Oh, all right, Charlie," she sighed, drooping back on to his shoulder. "I expect you know best."

"Now and then I do," admitted Charlie, gratified but wary.

"I expect she'd only be a trouble to you."

"If you ask me, she doesn't know what she's asking for."

"It's not like as if she was really a friend of yours, neither." Winnie sighed again. "I always say there isn't anything you wouldn't do for your friends."

"Not within reason there isn't," agreed Charlie, rendered incautious by the arrival of his next course.

A sudden light gleamed behind the pathos of Winnie's eyes.

"Then wouldn't you do this just for me?" she said plaintively. . . .

II

He gave way. Inevitably he gave way. When the party assembled at the corner Nina was there. She made no difference, however, to their number, for Henry was suffering from a slight cold, and had promised Pamela to go to bed early. His absence left Alistair in a peculiarly defenceless position, which Nina was quick to see and take advantage of for the rest of the boys, though not really impolite, were obviously unaffected by her refined good looks.

"It's such a comfort to have a *gentleman* with the party," she murmured, as soon as they had taken their places in the 'bus. "If I hadn't known *you* were coming, Mr. French, I b'lieve I'd have stayed at home."

"Hard cheese," said Charlie Coe, apparently to no one in particular. He was sitting just in front of them, and every now and then turned round to lend Alistair the support of a friendly wink. Farther than that he was not prepared to go.

"If it wasn't for Mr. Cribb," continued Nina, shooting a scathing glance over the back of the seat, "I could never have brought myself to come at all. I do so hate roughness. But you'll look after me, won't you, Mr. French?"

It was obvious, in any case, that no one else would, for as soon as they arrived at the hall Charlie and the boys began a series of ingenious maneuvers which ended in her being placed right at the end of the row, with Alistair in the next seat to act as a buffer for the rest of the party. This arrangement appeared to afford Mr. Coe considerable relief, and in that overflowing of the heart which so often accompanies a narrow escape he hailed a boy with a basket and stood apples all round.

Their places were in the second row, just opposite what they hoped would turn out to be Eddie's corner, and separated from the Standing Room Only by line on line of less distinguished seats. Alistair turned round to look behind him, and was at once struck by the extraordinary power of boxing—that essentially British sport—to attract every class of Hebrew. Lithe young bloods, paunchy veterans, antique-dealers and pawnbrokers from a hundred indigent thoroughfares, their shrewd or liquid eyes were the life of the crowd. One of them Alistair could hardly keep his eyes off, a great mountainous fellow bulging over the seat of his chair, and whose coffee-coloured skin was sleek as parchment. He was shabbily and dirtily dressed in a variety of second-hand clothes, and on the thumb of his right hand smouldered a big sullen ruby.

With an effort Alistair shifted his gaze and returned to the patrons of standing room. They were not a particularly athletic-looking lot. Here and there a heavy-shouldered youngster stood out from the ruck, and one or two of the older men looked pretty tough, but for the most part the type was light, sallow, and narrow across the chest. From the walls to the back row of chairs they were packed six or seven deep, moving little, speaking in clipped undertones, their faces curiously uniform between cap and twisted muffler; and it must have been this quiet uniformity, coupled with the doubtful lighting, that gave them an oddly insubstantial look, as of so many serried shadows waiting the next shout from Charon. There was nothing tenuous about the better-lit rows in front, where small tradesmen sat squarely in their places and shifted their feet with solemn courtesy when any one wanted to get by.

"Oh, dear," said Nina daintily, "whatever shall I do with the core?"

Alistair took it from her and dropped it under the seat in front. It was a wicker arm-chair, like all the others in that superior row, and they were occupied by the very sleekest of the Jews and young men whose shoulder-muscles rippled and bulged under the lily-gilding of padded jackets. These were the connoisseurs, the people who knew, and Alistair had never before seen so many cauliflower ears at the same time. Nor was the feminine charm lacking in this exclusive circle, for several of the heroes had brought their women-folk, ladies with flashing personalities and luxuriant furs. One in particular Alistair marked with admiration, whose ripe attractions (for they were all fine women rather than snappy cuties) were set off by a collar of red fox that rose a good inch above her tiny green hat. Besides a black and roving eye she had a habit of whacking her escort on the knee with a large crocodile-skin bag: he was one of the smaller Hebrews, and not at all the sort of man one would have expected to woo and win so stupendous a beauty.

"Want to see the program?" asked Charlie. Bought as they entered the hall, it had up till that moment been monopolized by Mr. Hickey. With rising excitement they scanned the list of fights—Sensational Fifteen rounds, Extra-special twelve, Thrilling ten, and then there it was in actual print: Interesting eight-rounds contest, Eddie Cribb (Paddington) *v.* Hackney Jack (Hackney.)

"Good old Eddie," said Charlie Coe.

The boys looked at each other solemnly, their rowdiness subdued to awe. Good old Eddie, they thought. Oh, *good* old Eddie, and cripes if he could only win it'd be worth a week's wages . . .

"He'll come on about third," surmised Charlie. "Welterweight, see? The first two'll be kids' stuff, most like. You ask me anything you want, Mr. French."

But Alistair had no questions, not even when Boy Cook and Young McKenna were knocking each other about the ring with all the enthusiasm of seventeen-year-old flyweights. The boxing was good enough of its kind, but what chiefly impressed him was one of the seconds, a little old man with a Phil May fringe and a face the colour of terra-cotta. It was his duty, while the other two slapped and sluiced, to fan his principal with a dirty towel; and this he did with an earnestness beyond all description. Legs straddled apart, head a little on one side, forehead wrinkled in a frown of concentration, he flapped and flapped as though with each sweep of the towel he drove fresh strength and cunning into the pulsing body spread-eagled before him. Alistair hoped Eddie was going to have that man.

The kids departed, one of them a victor on points, but both in very good spirits and cuffing each other amicably as they left the ring. The next pair were sterner stuff, Irish Maloney and Battling Harry Todd, two tough-grained sprigs of the true bruiser stock. They fought like a couple of young bulls, heads lowered, and with a plain animal brutality that roused the whole audience to vociferous life. If Alistair had had time to glance behind him he would have seen the shadowy ranks suddenly metamorphosed into so many hundred 'bus-conductors, messenger-boys, butchers, bakers, tobacconists, burglars, greengrocers, newsagents and ex-marines, all surging with the original and sinful joy of a bloody scrap. They groaned, they applauded, they shouted advice. The voice of the M.C. rose imperiously over the tumult, dominated it for a moment, and was lost again in the hurricane of sound.

"Box 'im, 'Arry!"

"Keep away from 'im, 'Arry!"

"Come on, Ireland!"

"Use yer left, 'Arry!"

"Get out of it, Ref.!"

"Get out of it, Ref., we can't see!"

Alistair thrilled to the voice of the crowd. He too shouted and beat his hands, and watched with passionate interest the sudden spurt of blood over Maloney's eye. It spread downwards like a red mask, blinding him so that he hit out wildly at the air, and an instant later, almost before the referee's decision, his seconds were into the ring. Irish Maloney retiring injured, Battling Harry Todd was declared winner.

"Ours next," said Charlie.

In the heat of the fight Alistair had almost forgotten. It seemed to him that the bout had only just ended, when suddenly the man in front of him turned in his chair, and there was Eddie Crib coming down the gangway in his old brown overcoat. He looked neither to right nor left, but straight ahead to the empty ring.

The sight, thrilling enough to the whole party, was altogether too much for one of them, and with a stifled cry Nina turned up her eyes and fell sideways in a dead faint. For a moment Alistair's excitement deadened the blow, and it was only when she remained in that position, instead of sitting up again, that he grasped what had happened. In natural horror, and warding her off with his right arm, he turned to Charlie Coe.

"I say, Nina's fainted!"

"Good," said Charlie.

He did not even look round, and Alistair realized with a sinking heart that he was not going to offer any assistance. Meanwhile Nina's whole weight was resting against his shoulder, and in another moment she would be more or less in his lap. With growing distress he passed his free arm behind Charlie's back and pulled Reg Bennett's sleeve.

"I say," he hissed hopefully (for the commissionaire was notoriously kind-hearted), "Nina's fainted."

Reggie whistled sympathetically.

"She ought to be taken out."

"That's right," agreed Charlie, without moving his eyes from the ring. "Long ago she ought . . ."

"We'll tell you all about it tomorrow," promised kind Mr. Bennett.

"If it was me," added Charlie, "I'd put her on the curb and come back."

There was nothing for it. With curses in his heart, Alistair first reached under the seat for his hat and coat, then held Nina off with one hand while he got up. As soon as he let go she fell forward, so that the people in the row behind were at a loss to account for her sudden disappearance; but this apparent bonelessness made her at least easier to carry. With the vigorous hoick known as a Fireman's Lift Alistair jerked the lovely burden on to his right shoulder, and thus encumbered began making his way towards the door. A good many things seemed to be dropping out of her pockets, but Alistair never stopped. No one took any notice, they were all too intent on the ring, and as he reached the passage Alistair heard a sudden roar of approval rise behind him. He would have liked to look back, but just then Nina began to wriggle feebly and instead he smothered his regrets and hurried out to the street.

III

It was fortunately a fine clear night, and hardly had he replaced her in an upright position when both eyes and mouth opened together.

"Why, wherever am I?" asked Nina, clutching at his coat in a loopy sort of way. "Has there been an accident?"

With commendable restraint Alistair explained the true circumstances of the case, adding that if she were feeling better they would soon be able to return: but the suggestion nearly sent her off again.

"Oh, I couldn't Mr. French," she implored him. "I couldn't bear it. I just want to go home."

Charlie's advice echoed in his ears, but he had not the courage to take it. Instead, after a short interval to let Nina get her strength, he not only accompanied her down Handel Street but was also forced to give her his arm. She clung like a leech.

"If she faints again," Alistair promised himself, "I'll just leave her in a doorway . . ."

But in the cool night air Nina rapidly revived, and was soon able to describe her various emotions at seeing Eddie Cribb clamber into the ring. They were so intense that really it was a wonder she was still alive, much less walking along Russell Street on a gentleman's arm.

"But that's me all over," explained Nina, leaning a little harder. "I'm so temperamental."

Loosening her grip by a sudden movement of the elbow, Alistair remarked that this was probably due to her work on the stage.

"Oh, it is. An actress without temperament—why, she may make a good reliable understudy, but she'll never be a star. And I'm an actress through and through, Mr. French, whatever I may appear at the present. Sometimes—it's not every one I could say this to, of course—sometimes, when I think of myself behind that counter, I can hardly believe it. Why, when I was in *Oh, Pepita!* Mr. Marks—he was the stage-manager, and a real artist—he said I could be another Gertie Millar if I'd only work." Nina broke off and sighed temperamentally. "But you know how it is when you're popular—dancing, night-clubs, supper-parties after the show—and me nothing more than a kid with no one to guide me. I wish I'd known *you* then, Mr. French."

"I wish you had too," said Alistair, at the same time accelerating his step.

Although she had previously been walking with comparative vigor, the sudden increase in pace (or it might have been a certain lack of response) now began to take its toll, and opposite the next taxi rank Nina forced to complain of returning giddiness; but Alistair felt he had already been gentlemanly enough for one night and hurried her on towards the 'bus stop.

"We'll soon be home," he said encouragingly, "I expect you've had a long day." Unfortunately the encouragement proved greater than he had anticipated, and she nestled into his shoulder with renewed interest.

"You're right there, Mr. French. No one knows what I suffer, on my feet from morning till night. I wonder why you're so kind to me?"

"Isn't every one kind to you?" countered Alistair rather cleverly.

"Oh, no." Nina shook her head from side to side, pathetic as a dying bluebell. Then she remembered her previous statement about the supper-parties, and added that the gayest life was not always the happiest. Men, for all their fine protestations, were always wanting something. . . .

"But you're not like that, are you, Mr. French?"

A new and disturbing thought suddenly occurred to him. He thrust it back, but with every second it took clearer shape. It was that Cressida and Nina both belonged to the same profession.

The parallel was of course ridiculous, but troubling nevertheless. Their different voices spoke in almost the same idiom. Or was it something even deeper than that, an attitude of mind, a constant preoccupation with managers and temperament? It was intolerable that his beautiful Cressida should have anything in common with this little outcast from the back row, and yet the notion persisted. "A good reliable understudy"—it was the very phrase for Cressida's exquisite irony. . . .

At this moment, and to his infinite relief, their 'bus swung round the corner, and in the excitement of hauling Nina on to the platform and shoving her into a seat he shook off the odd preoccupation. But not for long. All the way back to Bloom Street Alistair brooded in silence, neglecting at least three opportunities of holding Nina's hand, two in the 'bus, and another, even more promising, on the unlighted stairs of Number Fifteen. The Parker sitting-room was also in complete darkness, and she begged him to wait while she lit the gas.

"Winnie must have taken Ma to the pictures," said Nina, looking wistfully round the empty room. "I wonder if I shall feel lonely, all by myself,"

"You won't if you go straight to bed," said Alistair. "What you want is a long night's sleep." And with that he shut the door behind him and continued his way upstairs.

IV

The next morning was signalized by Winnie's bringing up the top-floor milk, taking away the empty bottle, and offering to make Alistair's bed. She was obviously suffering from considerable vicarious remorse, and hoped by these attentions to console him for having been done out of Eddie's victory. For he had won handsomely, with the only knock-out of the evening, and the referee had called him a young Dempsey.

"Charlie nipped in just now on his way to work," explained Winnie. "He said to tell you he was ever so sorry you missed it, because it was a very convincing display. Him and the boys was coming back last night, but they got a bit above themselves and he thought better not." The party, it seemed, had waited for Eddie at the door, and he came out and had chips with them, not a bit proud. They said Mr. Moss was ever so excited, much more excited than Eddie, who never turned a hair; but he told Charlie afterwards that until he got his feet on the canvas he was feeling sick as a cat.

Alistair listened with almost equal enthusiasm, finding something extraordinarily romantic in this first step in the assault on a World Championship. Winnie agreed with him.

"It's ever so queer, isn't it?" she said. "An', you know, I wouldn't be a bit surprised if he pulled it off. Charlie says he's never seen anything like it. He says the minute Eddie got into the ring he looked right where he ought to be—right at home like. And it takes a lot to startle Charlie."

When she had gone downstairs again Alistair picked up the milk, and with unusual deliberation set about making coffee. But the slowness of his movements was no index to the tempo of his thoughts. They raced, they churned, they rattled inside his head, set in perpetual motion by the talk on the landing.

He wished, with concentrated passion, that he had been a boxer.

CHAPTER XIX

I

ALTHOUGH at first somewhat overshadowed by the fore-going events, Henry's engagement was by no means forgotten, and a day or two later he was pressingly invited to bring his young lady to a ceremonial tea in the Parker sitting-room. It was a meal of great elegance, without ham, and attended only by the very best people. They were Winnie, Ma, Mr. Hickey, Nina (whose refinement added tone to the whole gathering), Charlie Coe, Eddie Cribb, and of course Alistair. Tea was laid on the large table, in the center of which, as a compliment to the happy couple, stood a plate of Garibaldi or squashed-fly biscuits surrounded by orange-blossoms. These, although artificial, were strongly scented, their perfume mingling agreeably with that of the fish-paste sandwiches.

"Ever so real, isn't it?" said Winnie, sniffing the laden air. "The label says guaranteed six months, but they only come in yesterday, so we can't tell."

"From the shop, are they?" asked Charlie Coe, not unimpressed.

Winnie nodded: she had borrowed them out of the flower department. (It was also her delicacy that had prevented Ma from putting them round the cherry cake instead of the biscuits. After all, it didn't want to look too like a wedding.)

With various expressions of delight the guests took their places. It was a perfect display of good behavior: Mr. Hickey extraordinarily affable, Charlie and Eddie silent but correct, the guests of honour friendly and pleasant with all. There was nothing, in fact, to mar the enjoyment except a slight anxiety as to what Ma Parker would say next. She was apparently under the impression that the wedding was to take place immediately, and that Henry would bring his bride home to the top floor; nor could any argument shake her conviction.

"*You'll* have to move out, young man," she told Alistair, selecting as always one of the rare pauses in the conversation. "They won't want *you* popping in and out . . ."

"Oh, come off it, Ma," called Winnie, "haven't I told you they're not coming here at all? You're bats, that's what's the matter with you!"

"And you want turning up and slapping, that's what's the matter with *you*," replied the old lady rapidly. "Nice way to talk to your elders!" She turned back to Alistair, and picked up the dropped thread of her conversation. "I lay you've 'ad a fine turn-out up there, 'aven't you, now? Photographs. . . . Pho, you needn't be ashamed of them." (Alistair was indeed scarlet, but for other reasons.) "I know what young gentlemen are like. The first year I was in London I used to do for a gentleman in them rooms by the river, and the pictures 'e 'ad! Naked women was nothing," She peered up at him inquisitively, for all the world like a wicked old parrot, a parrot that had been brought up on gin and sugar at some dock-side pub, "Young blood wasn't meant to freeze, that's what I say, and sometimes your eyes'll warm you when the blankets can't."

"Here, listen to this!" shrilled Winnie, "listen to what Eddie's wrote in my book!" She banged loudly on the table, flourishing a pink suède autograph album that one of the boys had given her for Christmas. "You listen too, Mr. Brough, it's ever so appropriate:

> 'Think of me on the ocean,
> Think of me on the lake,
> Think of me on your wedding day,
> And send me a piece of cake!'

There!"

The applause was deservedly great, Henry demanding to be provided with a copy, Pamela praising the meter, even Mr. Hickey admitting that he'd heard worse. As for Nina, her admiration was so overwhelming that for some minutes she could only gaze in silent wonder.

"Oh, I do like that," she sighed. "Oh, I *do* think that's clever. I'd like to learn it by heart."

Eddie Cribb wriggled uneasily. He had tried to stop Winnie reading the thing out, but she would do it, and this was what happened.

"Did you make it up yourself?" persisted Nina, yearning towards him. "Would you make another up for me, if I had a book?"

Eddie opened his mouth, but not quickly enough. Winnie had heard the tail-end of the question, and now rushed joyfully in to swell his triumph.

"Did you really, Eddie? Why didn't you never tell me? Here, Mr. Brough, Eddie made up that piece himself. Isn't he clever?"

"I say, did he really?" exclaimed Henry. "That's pretty bright. Pamela, d'you hear that Mr. Cribb—"

"It's so simple, that's what I like about it," said Nina, suddenly far more refined than any one else. She had begun to eat again, nibbling with the front teeth only at a Garibaldi biscuit; but her pale-blue eyes were still glazed with admiration.

"Ever see a dying cod?" whispered old Ma Parker loudly.

Even as he pretended not to hear Alistair wondered for which of his sins he had been placed next to this awful old woman. To make matters worse, Mr. Hickey, sitting on her other side, had by this time exhausted his stock of sociability and relapsed into complete silence, so that all her attention was now concentrated on Alistair alone.

"I s'pose the next thing we know," she said jovially, "you'll be bringing 'ome a young woman yourself. Maybe you've got your eye on 'er already?"

"No such luck," replied Alistair, keeping up his courage with a bloater-paste sandwich.

"Ah, well, I don't say you're not right to take your time. Put a bit of flesh on first, that's what I always say." She squinted round at him with a noiseless chuckle. "But you wait till they're up there billing and cooing like a couple o' turtles, and then see if you don't change your mind."

"I hardly think so," mumbled Alistair, considerably shocked by the sight of such frank and ribald enjoyment in so aged an eye. "Besides, you know, you've got it wrong about Mr. Brough. They aren't going to be here at all."

"Not for long they won't," agreed Ma Parker. "That's what *I* say. Not after the first year." At the other end of the table Henry was talking very loudly about the new film at the Yellow Domes, but she merely raised her voice to a throaty cackle and continued unheeding: "They'll be wanting a garden for the pram. Poor thing, she doesn't know what she's in for."

"Here, have some of this," said Alistair, reaching for the cherry cake. "Do let me cut you a piece. It looks ripping."

"Not for me, thank you. I find it lays too 'eavy on the stomach." Old Ma Parker shook her head regretfully and returned to her original topic. "One thing, though, they'll get a good welcome 'ome, 'ere, that I will see too. . . ."

The sunken mouth puckered into a grin, the beady eyes sparkled, her whole aged countenance was suddenly alive with that pure bawdy gusto that makes some parts of Shakespeare so unsuitable for the use of schools. She dug Alistair sharply in the ribs.

"Tie a bell under the bed," said old Ma Parker.

It was nearly seven when the party broke up—or rather when Henry, Pamela and Alistair came away; for the rest of the company had settled down for a game of rummy and seemed unlikely to separate before midnight. As the door closed behind him, indeed, and with the noise of cheerful voices sounding through its thin panels, Alistair rather regretted his precipitance; especially on realizing that he would now have to turn out and go for a walk. The evening was rather unpleasant than otherwise, but he had eaten too much to face the Riviera, and since Henry and Pamela had already nipped upstairs there seemed to be no alternative.

He had just come to this conclusion and was preparing to go hatless into the night, when the door behind him opened, and Charlie Coe came out.

"Here, about that piece of poetry," said Charlie.

Alistair showed a natural bewilderment.

"Think o' me on the ocean think o' me on the lake," resumed Charlie rapidly. "That one. Eddie never wrote it at all."

"But I thought Winnie said—"

"Winnie, she got hold of the wrong end of the stick. Eddie never wrote it, he copied it out of a book his sister had. He just told me."

And having thus removed the stain from his friend's character Charlie nodded pleasantly and returned to his game.

Feeling slightly lonelier than before Alistair continued his way downstairs and reached the hall without further interruption. While they had been at the party the post must have come in, for Arnold Comstock was stooping over the mat picking up some letters.

"One for you an' one for Mr. Brough," he said, turning them over to look at the backs.

Alistair held out his hand, but without the usual stirring of curiosity. Henry's would be from a scholastic agency, his own from Aunt Gertrude: both would keep.

But he turned out to be only half-correct, for while one was indeed from Messrs. Gabbitas and Thring, the other, addressed to himself, bore not the least resemblance to Aunt Gertrude's diffident missives. The envelope, bright blue in colour, was a long narrow rectangle, covered all over with a pattern of flowing curves which when looked at very quickly resolved themselves into his address. Completely forgetful of Arnold Comstock, conscious only of an overwhelming excitement, Alistair sat down on the stairs and slit it open.

It was a letter from Camilla Dane.

It said:

17 Old Bruton Street.
April 3.

DEAR ALISTAIR FRENCH,—

Come to my party on Wednesday will you Wednesday week. Any time after eleven-thirty.

Yours,
CAMILLA DANE.

That was all, but it was enough for Alistair. In any case she could not have squeezed another word into the page. With something between a sob and a shout of joy he flung the envelope into the air, clapped Mr. Comstock violently on the back, and rushed out to propose to Cressida.

II

Half-way down the road, of course, he remembered that he had no hat, that his hands were dirty, and that she was going to the theatre; and owing to these and other considerations it was not till a day and a half later that they met by appointment in Kensington Gardens. Familiarity with the local fauna had led Alistair to fix the rendezvous for one o'clock, by which hour all efficient nursemaids were shepherding their charges home for lunch, and he anticipated no difficulty in finding a suitably private proposing-ground.

But Cressida, usually indifferent to real scenery, for once exhibited a strong preference for the shores of the Serpentine, and accordingly they set off towards the bridge. She was in one of her gentler, more youthful moods, sniffing delightedly at the young grass and drawing her companion's attention to the many shades in a green tree. But Alistair did not respond as rapturously as might have been expected: it had just struck him that though the orthodox nurses had disappeared, their place was more than filled by the bread-and-jam contingent from the Harrow Road. One little girl of about ten, with true feminine flair, was already shadowing them at a distance of about four feet; and since she was accompanied by three younger children her presence seemed an almost certain source of future embarrassment.

"Headache, my dear?" asked Cressida gently.

And as if that were not enough ravishment, she then gave him the perfect opening by asking whether he could take her to Olga's flat-warming on Wednesday week.

"'Fraid I can't," said Alistair. "Camilla Dane's got a party, and I've promised to go."

In the ten seconds before she found words he tasted all the joys of achievement.

"My dear! How marvellous! Does she want to see you about the play?"

"I rather gathered so." The lie slipped out with all the naturalness of unpremeditation. "She seems to be no end keen on it."

"How much is actually written now?"

"Oh, practically the lot. With any luck, I shall be able to take it along to the party and deposit it in person."

Once more, after all those months, her eyes admired him.

"But that's splendid, darling! I was afraid you were getting on to a bad patch."

"I was a bit," Alistair admitted. "At the beginning of last month I couldn't write a word." He was now inventing recklessly, tasting almost for the first time the intellectual freedom that results from a frank renunciation of the truth. "As a matter of fact, nearly all the early stuff has been scrapped—Markham didn't much care for it, you remember—and I came to the conclusion that he was right. After all, he's had a good deal of experience . . ."

"I do think you're so sensible," said Cressida approvingly. "People who won't alter a word never get anywhere. When did you begin to rewrite?"

Hastily computing the shortest possible time in which a play could be rewritten, he replied with nonchalance, about a fortnight ago; and added that although it was notoriously difficult to judge one's own work, some of the dialogue had struck him as really rather good.

"There's a scene on a balcony," he said, "which has a sort of poetic quality running all through it—not just the usual moons and nightingales, but something more elusive. She'll never play that scene as well as you could."

"But she'll get you far more publicity," said Cressida practically. "I'll wait for the first revival . . ."

In this absorbing conversation they had reached the bridge, and now stood a moment leaning on the parapet. The little girl halted too, and bade her three charges take a look at the boats.

"How queer it all is," said Cressida suddenly.

Alistair looked sideways at her, desperately wondering what she would like him to say. She was wearing a very sensible hat, so small as to cover hardly any of her hair, and thus gazing he presently forgot to speak at all. The uncounted minutes slid by and still they leant in silence, until at the same moment, by tacit consent, they began to walk across the bridge and back into the Gardens.

A sweet and pastoral mood descended on them, a happy quiet at last recaptured. Alistair remembered the first night of all, when they had walked together through the Bloomsbury squares, and how there had been no need to tell her of the fallen leaf, the shadow grenadier. The months between melted away, it might have been next morning.

"The sea-gulls are all gone," said Cressida.

Alistair nodded. He too regretted the white flotillas, and this startling conjunction of tastes seemed so miraculous that he would have proposed at once but for the inopportune proximity of a gentleman feeding sparrows. They walked on, loitering companionably to look at the pheasant, and presently came to the four stone-rimmed pools at the head of the Serpentine. Here Alistair, remembering the convenient embrasures of the balustrade over the water, quickened his pace a little, and led her to a secluded angle whence one looked straight down into the sparse leafage of a tall water plant. Black among the light-green stems, pretty as a Chinese picture, rode a small bird with a red-splashed beak. Cressida admired it greatly, and demanded its name.

"I think it's a moor-hen," said Alistair.

Glancing over his shoulder, he saw that the little girl with the pram had at last succeeded in tearing herself away, nor was the man feeding sparrows any longer in sight. He pulled himself together.

"And what's the one in the reeds?" asked Cressida.

Her face, bent a little above the water, was so unbearably lovely that his throat contracted with emotion and left him incapable of speech. He tried to say, "A duck," but though his lips moved well enough, nothing came out of them but a strangled gasp. Cressida half-turned, still thinking (as was evident from the beautiful composure of her brows) exclusively about water-fowl.

"On the Round Pond," she said, "there are some little black ones with yellow eyes. Let's go and see them."

Alistair shook his head. The fog in his throat seemed to have settled in a solid ball, so heavy that he could feel it thudding up and down in time to his heart. He swallowed painfully, and heard with relief the rasp of his returning voice.

"Cressida," he whispered.

This time she turned completely, and in her awakened eyes he saw a quiet attention, grave and innocent, that gave him nevertheless a feeling of being very . . . very young. Young and green.

"Cressida!"

It seemed as though he could find nothing else to say, only her name repeated over and over again. Cressida, Cressida! Love didn't make you eloquent, it drowned your five wits like so many blind kittens, delivered you dumb and helpless into the hands of the enemy. Cressida! . . . What else was there to say? And besides in the face of that quiet wisdom—what need?

"I expect you know already," said Alistair.

Then he remembered Winnie's injunctions, and added rather clumsily: "I—I want you to marry me."

For the hundredth time he noted the extreme beauty of her lashes, not thick, but so long and fine as to cast a delicate shadow on the smooth, faintly-coloured skin. In the contemplation of such loveliness years would pass like seconds, leaving a man still in the first flush of wonder. That must be what eternity was like. To stand like this, close enough to see the very grain of her cheek, was such bliss that he hardly wished for anything beyond; but as the seconds passed, and still she did not speak, he began to despair and curse his presumption. For after this, naturally, she would never wish to see him again.

"Cressida!"

Then marvellously, incredibly, she moved a step closer, and seeing her so near he forgot despair. For a moment they stood motionless, till at last the strange wisdom faded from her eyes, and she slid her ungloved hand into his; at which precise instant there sprang up four beautiful white fountains, a happy compliment in the best classical tradition, but due, in this case at least, to the tact and punctuality of His Majesty's Office of Works.

"It must be two o'clock," said Cressida.

CHAPTER XX

I

So ALISTAIR became the luckiest man in the world; and was surprised to discover, in the course of a day or two, that it did not make him particularly happy. His new official status brought no change in their relations—except the trifling one that Cressida now called him darling as a regular thing, instead of only once or twice an hour. The endearment was naturally welcome; but he knew she still went out frequently with other suitors.

"But, darling," said Cressida, laying her hand against his temple (it was one of her favourite gestures, light and swift as the caress of a swallow's wing)—"but, darling, I must dance sometimes. It's good for me. You know I'd much rather go with you, if we could . . ."

There it was. "If you could afford to take me to the Savoy, I should naturally prefer your company. But I can hardly be expected to give up my dancing merely because you are incapable of earning any money." Alistair admitted the reason of her attitude, even while he suffered under it. He now realized, too, how ludicrously mistaken had been Winnie's diagnosis. Fond or not fond—what had that to do with it? Cressida had accepted him, but did that make him any more sure of her affection? In a tender mood she would lean hours together with her head against his shoulder, until it seemed as though their love had isolated them from the rest of the world in a bubble of quiet happiness; and then just as he was going she would take down her silver ball-dress and unwrap the tissue paper. You couldn't tell.

About this time too, and as an additional complication, Alistair began to taste the disadvantages of sharing one room, however larger with an engaged couple. Especially when one of the couple was Pamela.

Except for the short period from midnight to 8 A.M. there was no hour at which he could feel secure from her irruption; and even more than this ubiquity he resented her perfectly absurd attitude towards Henry. Old Henry was undoubtedly one of the best, and had many excellent qualities; but to regard him as a sucking genius was simply fantastic. She moreover persisted (and this a bare five minutes after Henry had quitted the room) in referring, to him as very good-looking.

"Not exactly *handsome*, of course," she once told Alistair, "but so nice and strong. When we did *The Devil's Disciple* every one said he looked like a young Roman."

To which the obvious reply was that any one who looked like a young Roman in *The Devil's Disciple* must be a damned bad actor; but Alistair restrained himself. Pamela was sitting in the only comfortable chair waiting for Henry to come back with some Virginian cigarettes. It was raining steadily, and as soon as he returned Alistair knew that he himself would be forced to plunge into the downpour. In bad weather—and it was one of the wettest springs on record—he and Mr. Puncher sat side by side in the Free Library for hours on end, but whereas Mr. Puncher and his tin whistle always left at five (being due outside the Criterion at a quarter to six), Alistair usually stayed on till ten. If Cressida were going out there was nothing else to do, for he did not wish to spend money by himself; and in the nine days which elapsed between his proposal and the night of Miss Dane's party she went out six times.

On this party he now pinned all his hopes. It was to be the turning-point in his life; from which would date a new era of unparalleled industry and regular inspiration. For he had been getting—Alistair admitted it bravely—a trifle slack. He had allowed Henry and Pamela to drive him from his desk. It should never occur again, or at any rate—for he was even then tramping doggedly along the Embankment—never after next Wednesday. Turning up his coat collar against the wind (as usual it was coming on to rain), Alistair planned how he would draw Miss Dane aside at the first opportunity and convince her that his play, which would be finished within the fortnight, was going to be one of the masterpieces of the twentieth century. He saw the great brown eyes widen with delight, the scarlet lips part in wonder, and himself, basking in the limelight of her smiles, introduced to the admiring party as a coming dramatist. After that he would jolly well have to finish it.

There was another reason, too, why Alistair looked forward with such passion to the late hours of Wednesday night. He was wondering whether Raymond Paget had also been invited.

The inexplicable collapse of their friendship had never ceased to puzzle him, and even with his mind full of Cressida he had now and then gone back to the Albert Memorial to see if by any chance the artist were there. But the Memorial, like the Embryo Club, appeared to be a place where everybody is seen once in their lives and never again. It was of course quite possible that Mr. Paget had gone abroad, or was busy working; but though the ingenious devices of telephone and post card seemed expressly designed to help him find out, Alistair never availed himself of either.

For six hours, roughly, they had been on terms of closest, most exciting intimacy: within that time the whole course of his life had been radically altered: and the next day there was nothing at all. Even now it was with a flush of discomfort that Alistair recalled his letter of thanks written the following morning, no more than two or three lines scribbled off in light-hearted anticipation of their next meeting, and which had never received a reply. A similar, though slightly more formal note had gone to Miss Dane, with the same result. That was perhaps only to be expected in view of her many preoccupations; and yet—and yet. . . .

They had both seemed to like him.

For all his boastful dreaming Alistair was not really conceited. The offer, or what he took to be the offer, of Raymond Paget's friendship had filled him with astonished gratitude: in the presence of Camilla Dane his natural instinct was to adore and efface himself: but it was they who had hauled him from his knees into a position of equality. With something like awe Alistair remembered how he had helped himself to champagne and folded an ermine cloak round the star's shoulders. If she hadn't been so gracious he could never have done it, any more than he could have written that confiding and imbecile note to Raymond Paget. They were like people who adopted a stray puppy and then got tired of it after half a day.

Alistair pulled himself up sharply, aghast at such ingratitude. Was not Miss Dane's invitation actually in his pocket? And had not Mr. Paget spoken almost continuously of foreign travel? He was probably somewhere in Italy, or Venice, or perhaps Egypt, making masterly sketches of things like Cleopatra's Needle, which Alistair happened to be passing at that very moment. You couldn't expect a man like that to remember the address of every budding playwright in London. Only it would be nice if he got back just in time to open Camilla's invitation and leap into a taxi and meet his young friend on the doorstep. . . .

There was no use in worrying, Wednesday would settle everything; only it sometimes seemed to Alistair that Wednesday would never come.

II

In this, however, he was wrong. Exactly eleven days after he received the invitation April 15 dawned in a slight drizzle, cleared up after lunch, and at eight o'clock, when Alistair began to get ready, encouraged him with the sight of dry pavements. It was the first time since coming to Bloom Street that he had put on evening clothes, and the piquancy of such a toilet was heightened by the fact that Henry was already in bed.

"But I shall still be awake when you come in," he promised. "I'm going to go through all my history notes since the beginning of the year." It was rather a nice thing of Henry to do, for he needed a lot of sleep himself and disapproved of late nights in others; but for once the importance of the occasion seemed to have percolated through his natural defences.

"I do wish I had tails," said Alistair, standing on a chair to inspect his creases. "I'd have got them last year if it hadn't been for Aunt Gertrude."

"I've a white waistcoat you can borrow if you like," said Henry. "It's in the bottom part of my trunk."

"Not with a dinner-jacket, old man. But thanks all the same."

"Well, the Prince of Wales does," retorted Henry.

"It's different for the Prince of Wales," said Alistair, getting off the chair and taking a look at his tie. "Every one would know he'd done it on purpose. With me it's got to be one thing or the other, and that means it's got to be a dinner-jacket. The thing I am glad about is my hat."

He picked up the black felt lying ready on the table, and after a religious brushing tried it on before the glass. With the addition of a white silk muffler the effect was dashing in the extreme. He thought it made him look rather like a film star.

"You can have my bowler if you like," said Henry.

Not for the first time Alistair wondered how on earth they had managed to live together so long. But it was kindly meant, and he replied gently:

"Thanks awfully, old man, but I'd have to stick my ears out to keep it on. You must have an awful lot of brain."

Henry bore the disappointment with his usual stoicism, and began settling himself comfortably for the approaching vigil. On a chair by the bed were arranged several thick exercise-books containing History Notes, a volume on England in the Fourteenth Century, and two bars of nut-milk chocolate. In order to save the fire and in case he wanted to sit up he wore a thick white sweater over his pyjamas. On the floor, but within easy reach, lay a pipe, tobacco-pouch, and match-box. The sight of all these dispositions made Alistair feel he was going to be away a very long time.

"Don't try and stay awake all night, old man," he said rather anxiously. "You've to be at college in the morning."

Henry nodded agreeably and reached for his notes.

"Look here, I'll leave the door open and then if the light's out I'll know to come in quietly."

"Right you are," said Henry, opening his book at the Wars of the Roses.

With a last look in the mirror Alistair assumed his overcoat and made a rapid survey of door-key, money, and pocket-handkerchief. They were all in their places. He then bade farewell to Henry, returned, after a moment's hesitation, to borrow an extra half-crown, and at last took himself off to meet his fate.

III

On the floor below Winnie lay awake thinking of her red coat. Her feeling towards the garment was now definitely proprietary and almost solemnly joyful; for in another week it would be hers at last. Tucked under the lining paper of the bureau drawer were three pound notes and a two-shilling piece: as soon as she got paid the Friday after next she could go straight along and have it out of the window.

Luxuriantly she arranged the details. Her own shop shut at six, whereas Madame Louise kept open till seven; so there would be ample time to nip back to Bloom Street and collect Nina and the money. Nina's shop shut at six, too, but she didn't like meeting outside places, she said she was always being spoken to—a sign of delicacy which Winnie admired very much indeed. Anyway, Nina was much nearer home to start with, and would probably want to do her face. . . .

At this point her reflections were interrupted by the sound of some one running downstairs. One of the boys on the top, thought Winnie. A funny time to go out, though; must be well after eleven! Or perhaps it was only to post a letter. . . . For some minutes she lay still as a mouse, listening for the return; but all was silent. The incident, however, had effectually aroused her curiosity and by the time she finally got to sleep Alistair was knocking at a door in New Bruton Street.

CHAPTER XXI

I

SOME one gave him a drink, and as soon as he could get rid of his coat he plunged boldly into the stream of new arrivals and came up gasping not far from the grand piano. There some one gave him a drink, and he presently caught sight of his hostess lying in a huge green chair on the other side of the room. He tried to go and speak to her, and might even have succeeded in doing so but for a very beautiful girl with red hair who had unfortunately dropped her bag. Common courtesy compelled him to his knees until it was discovered under a large and popular *comédienne*, and by that time the green chair was empty save for two young men and a girl called Chloe. The girl with the bag was married, and her grateful husband had no difficulty in finding Alistair a drink; only after that they unfortunately had to go on, and he was just setting out once more in search of Miss Dane when all movement was brought to a standstill by a young girl who said she hoped everybody with any morals would leave the room before she began to sing. So Alistair took up a good position against a piece of modern decoration, but it was rather disappointing.

Then some one gave him a drink, and he began dancing with a girl called Stella who ran a book-shop in a converted garage near Theobald's Road. All the books had been banned, so that the police made monthly raids disguised as intelligentsia, and this would have been very trying had she not found a way to buy them off with pornographic post cards and cups of tea. Alistair in return told her a good deal about himself, and they agreed that Life was nothing save as a means to an end. She also told him a very interesting story about a friend of hers, a girl with a delightful sense of humour who had an illegitimate child the previous summer, and after six months, being completely broke, decided to go home. So she waited for the first snowy day, and turned up at dusk wearing a red velvet dress and with the infant wrapped in a shawl, *just* like the melodramas, but unfortunately her father never saw the joke, and having revived her with Oxo dispatched her forthwith to a local mission. So then Alistair had another drink or two and danced with a girl called

Jimmy. But they didn't get on very well, and by the time he came back with their gins she had gone to powder her nose, so he gave one of them to a young man about his own age who had just brought out a book of verse and promised to send Alistair a signed copy. They exchanged addresses, but discovering, in the course of further conversation, that they both came from Norbury, soon drifted apart. About this time Alistair began to be conscious of a slight depression, and would have been pleased to discuss the ultimate aims of civilization; but instead some one gave him a drink and introduced him to a girl called Petronella.

She was very beautiful, and Alistair might seriously have considered marrying her but for her annoying trick of screaming with laughter whenever he opened his mouth. On the way to the buffet, however, she clung very sweetly to his arm, and he exerted himself to fetch her a lobster patty. For some reason the thought of food made no appeal to him personally, though he accepted a drink from a rather charming little man who had just been on tour in Australia. Alistair took him back to Petronella, but she had to go and powder her nose, and the two friends were left alone with a plate of broken meats.

"I shouldn't eat that stuff if I were you," advised the man from Australia, "it corrodes the liver."

"I wasn't thinking of it," said Alistair, warmly. He didn't want a row, but there were limits.

Then some one gave him a drink, and a whole party of them sat down to play hunt-the-slipper. It was very comfortable on the floor, only people would stretch their legs out to the middle instead of keeping them tucked under in the proper position. A pale-pink slipper struck Alistair sharply on the cheek, and with calm but angry dignity he rose to his feet and sat down on a convenient sofa. There some one gave him a drink, and the girl with the red hair (who after all hadn't gone on with her husband) said it was a shame. She also said that she had had about enough of this party, and asked where he lived, Alistair told her, and she said they might as well split a taxi. So they had another drink and went down by the stairs, because the lift looked rather unsafe, and found a cab. But at Oxford and Cambridge Terrace she kissed him absently and got out, leaving Alistair to count his sixpences all the way to Bloom Street.

II

Before he was half-way upstairs the door on the top landing opened and a round bullet-head appeared over the banisters. It was Henry, wide awake at three in the morning to hear about the party.

"Well?" he called softly. "What was it like?"

"Oh, marvellous," replied Alistair, "absolutely marvellous . . ."

And with a laugh of gay reminiscence he turned aside into the lavatory and was sick.

CHAPTER XXII

I

THE next seven days were the unhappiest of Alistair's life. The morning after the party he telephoned Cressida at the café where they were to have met for lunch, canceling the appointment and explaining that he would be invisible for a week. He had a new idea, an absolute winner, which Miss Dane had urged him to get on to paper without delay, and he knew Cressida would forgive him.

Cressida forgave him. Then she too became invisible.

The first day he stood it pretty well, being almost completely occupied in treating his headache. But the second was terrible, and on the third he went round to Carey Street at his usual hour. Cressida was out He resisted the temptation to leave a message and came back. That night, in desperation, he did actually begin a new play, which was to combine a leading part for Camilla Dane with a secondary but no less striking part for Cressida herself; and falling into a vein of poetic prose he wrote several love scenes with great rapidity. On reading them over in the morning, however, their badness was so patent that he lost heart and shelved the whole thing.

It was about this time, too, that Henry began to harp on the subject of giving up their room. He had got his post at Willesden, and hoped to be married early in September: so that there was no point in his keeping it on a day after the end of the term. But he showed a very friendly regard for Alistair's convenience, and had no wish to hustle him out.

"Only as soon as you *can* let me have a date," he said, "I'll see about giving notice. This weekly business is darned useful."

That was Henry all over, thoughtful, good-tempered, unselfish, even when in love. He had behaved well, too, over the party, apparently accepting at its face value Alistair's carefully edited account, and refraining from all further inquiry. No one could have been easier to live with, and Alistair disliked him exceedingly.

He was also beginning to be seriously worried about his finances. The rigid economy of the first few months had gradually been undermined by a spirit of reckless extravagance, and ever since Christmas—ever since he had known Cressida, almost—he had been living at the rate of at least two pounds fifteen a week; as a result of which his bank balance, with a third of the year yet to run, was now just under twenty pounds. During eight months in Bloom Street he had earned nothing at all.

In the drawer of the writing-table lay the draft of *Luna Park*, the draft of his novel, and the draft of his comedy of manners. He saw his mistake, of course: he should have concentrated on the more popular, more readily salable forms of literature, such as the short story and the bright article. That was the way to make money.

"Oh, damn money!" thought Alistair, like many a good man before him. "It's not as though I wanted much, only just enough . . ."

Something in the phrase tickled his memory. He seemed to recollect having thought those words before, but in a different connection, and a long time ago. Alistair frowned, casting his mind back to the early days of their migration, trying to fit a background to the modest sentiment. "Not much, only just enough . . ."

"Only just enough . . ."

"Just enough to live on . . ."

All at once he remembered the Embryo Club. The Embryo Club, a little old lady in a black coat, another old lady who had brought her needlework . . . and a youngster who had sat there despising the entire company. He had thought they all looked as though they had just enough to live on.

"Lucky devils," thought Alistair.

II

It usually took Winnie about twenty minutes to get home from work, but on this particular Friday, and having trotted all the way down Kimberly Street, she was back at Number Fifteen by ten past six. The exertion, however, had resulted in a stitch, forcing her to pause a moment at the gate while she got her breath: but for which accident she might never have noticed a man and a girl standing a few houses farther down. They were so withdrawn into the shadow that only the eyes of love could have recognized Arnold Comstock's gaunt height. Winnie hesitated. Her first impulse was to go and join them with a few words of badinage: but the novelty of seeing Arnold talking to a girl held her a few moments longer.

"It's a funny thing, me loving him like I do," thought Winnie simply.

She could feel her love like a physical pain, a dull sweet ache just over the heart. Charlie and the boys all said he was no good, but it didn't seem to matter. Only it seemed like as if he didn't care for girls at all . . . didn't seem to notice them like. That day at the baker's, f'rinstance. The sweet dull ache sharpened to almost unbearable poignancy. You couldn't do nothing with a boy like that.

But now one of the figures was moving, and the next instant Arnold had bent forward and was covering the face and throat of the girl with greedy kisses.

III

How she got away from the gate and into the house Winnie never knew, but presently, after what seemed like hours of slow climbing, she found herself sitting on the stairs just below the third-floor landing.

She was not capable of any emotion save the overwhelming need for solitude; and since Ma and Nina were both waiting for her there was nowhere else to be. But it wasn't bad there. In some curious way the edge of the next stair digging into her back was even a sort of help. Took her mind off things for a minute. Took her mind off Arnold.

Arnold!

Whoever would have thought it of him? Kissing a girl in the street, right in front of the house, and him so down on the pictures even! Why, time and again last summer, when she and the boys got larking about outside, he'd looked at them fair disgusted. Made Charlie ever so wild it did, and once he went and jostled him into the gutter all the way down the road. But Arnold being a Pacifist nothing had come of it. . . . Just full of ideals he was—Pacifist and Communist and that thing that met on Sunday mornings to talk about the failure of religion. And never so much as looking at a girl from one year's end to the other. Or so they'd thought. . . .

At this point some one wanted to come upstairs, and she had to get out of the way. It was one of the top-floor boys, the one who wrote things, but luckily he didn't stop and speak to her. Winnie watched him turn the corner and then sat down again.

And now a new wretchedness assailed her. It was all very well to know Arnold wasn't like what she'd thought, but suppose she had to go on being fond of him just the same? Hastily examining the state of her emotions (much as a man feels himself over after an accident) Winnie discovered, with a sinking heart, that such was indeed the case.

"I'm in for it all right," thought Winnie.

Without much success she tried to remind herself how none of the boys had ever liked him, and how even Mr. Hickey had sometimes passed remarks. Men never did have much use for the long weedy sort, she'd often noticed it. And as for manners! Why, he didn't know enough to walk on the outside of the curb. Even Sid Mason knew that, and look what a little squit he was. . . .

But it was no good. Weedy and ignorant though he might be, there was something about him against which all her criticism was powerless. He was Arnold. Besides, he wanted feeding up, and how could you expect a boy to behave right when he never had no one to learn him? (Not like Jim at the chemist's, who came from a good home and had every advantage. That was different.) Arnold, he only wanted taking in hand and he'd be as good as any of them. That girl he'd got outside—you could see with half an eye *she* wasn't the sort to be any help. Only why—why hadn't he come to some one who was? Some one who'd brisk him up and make a man of him? In spite of all her efforts the tears began to fall . . .

Winnie pulled herself together. This was no way to carry on, sitting and snivelling like a kid with the toothache. The thing to do was to behave like as if nothing was wrong, and then perhaps she'd feel better. Think of Nina, and the beautiful coat they were going to buy. Think of the lovely spotty fur. If she didn't get a move on Nina would think she'd gone and got run over.

She got up and ascended the last few steps. There wasn't a light on the landing, but Nina might have lit the gas; so before opening the door she carefully arranged her face in a cheerful smile. The precaution, however, proved super-fluous, for the room was empty.

Her first thought was that Nina must have got tired of waiting and gone out. She sat down on the edge of the ottoman, despair settling like a cope of lead on her narrow shoulders. It would be ever so nice to die. She rolled over on to her face, but the broken spring bruised her chest, and thrust her upright.

"Here, be your age," Winnie adjured herself: and rising stiffly to her feet she went over to the glass. Funny. Apart from a little smudging round her eyes she didn't look so bad. It was too much trouble to do her lashes again, but instead she reached for the rouge-pot and rubbed on some extra colour. *Beautiful Woman* was quite right, a lot depended on how you were looking.

Then there was the coat. She must go out to Madame Louise and buy the red coat, the red coat that she had wanted so long and saved up so faithfully for. It had a collar of leopard-skin, Winnie reminded herself, and big cuffs to match: with a coat like that any girl ought to be happy. She pictured herself strolling into the Riviera and all of them turning to look—Mr. Hickey and Charlie and the upstairs boys and Arnold.

Arnold!

"Oh, God," cried Winnie aloud, "why've I got to keep remembering?"

The sound of her own voice shocked and alarmed her. People who talked to themselves were starting to go mad, every one knew that. But perhaps once didn't count, only when it grew to be a habit. If only Nina had been there it wouldn't have happened.

And thinking of Nina, it now struck her that her friend might have misunderstood the arrangements, and gone straight to Madame Louise—in which case she would have been waiting ever so long—half an hour almost! And her with her dread of being spoken to! The bare possibility of such an imbroglio swamped all Winnie's other distresses in a wave of passionate remorse, and with renewed energy she snatched up her bag and flew to the bureau drawer.

The money was not there.

Winnie pulled out the drawer and tipped its contents on to Nina's bed. The money was not there. Then she looked slowly round the room, taking in for the first time its unaccustomed neatness. There were no undergarments lying about the floor, no stockings trailing from the towel-rail. One garter she did indeed pick up behind the washstand, but it was her own, left there the night before. She pulled aside the cretonne curtain that served as their wardrobe, and behind which Nina's dresses hung in the new moth-proof bag. They were gone, bag and all.

Still clutching her garter Winnie dropped the curtain and fled weeping from the room.

CHAPTER XXIII

I

ALISTAIR had passed Winnie on the stairs without noticing anything in the least unusual. One often found her sitting in odd places, and he was not in any case in an observant mood. Ever since the night of Camilla Dane's party he had been going about in a state of suspended animation, too unhappy to think, almost too unhappy to move. It was like a physical paralysis, numbing even the simplest faculties: he found it difficult, for example, to think what to say to people, and would hesitate minutes on end before crossing the road.

"It can't go on like this," thought Alistair.

He had just been to see Cressida, and for the fifth time in succession had found her out. That meant he hadn't seen her for over a week; and the lack of her was beginning to be like a dull pain underlying all his other ills.

It wasn't her fault. He had said, over the telephone, "You won't see me for a week"; and after that naturally she couldn't be expected to wait in for him. Besides, what had he to tell her when they did meet? That he had sat five days opposite a sheet of paper, and left it blank as he found it? That he was rapidly coming to the end of his money, and was apparently incapable of earning any more? Far better not see her at all, at any rate until the news was more promising. . . .

But there was an ache at his temples where she used to lay her hand.

Alistair reached the top landing and pushed open the door. In the big easy chair lay Cressida asleep.

It was like a load suddenly lifted from his shoulders, leaving him so light that for a moment he had to hold on to the door. Then he closed it softly behind him, and slipping off his overcoat tiptoed to her side. It was the first time he had seen her sleeping face.

The fine black lashes lay quite still, the curving mouth never moved: pride, ambition, love, all were gone with the colour from her cheeks, leaving a white purity that checked his heart.

He thought: "Where have you gone to, Cressida?"

Her forehead was so sweet and holy that he was afraid to kiss it. Drooping over the cushions her long hands were the hands of a saint. All the lines of her body slept in virginal calm. With the gesture of his own innocence Alistair knelt down and laid his head in her lap.

"Oh God . . ." he prayed.

A cool hand was laid at his temple, just where the pain was. He reached up and kissed it.

"I've been asleep," said Cressida.

A long ripple of returning life passed through her body. Alistair sat back on his heels so that he could see her wake.

"What time is it? I feel as though I'd been asleep hours."

"Only six," he told her. "Cressida . . ."

"Well?" the red lips parted in a final yawn, the black lashes flickered against her cheek. "Well, my dear?"

"It's so long since I've seen you," said Alistair.

"A week. But I wanted to see you too."

She spoke seriously, almost with embarrassment, so that instead of ecstasy he felt a sudden alarm, and with something like terror he saw her eyes, under his beseeching gaze, turn to grey ice. She said:

"Darling, I've got to talk to you. Do get up off the floor."

Silently Alistair obeyed. The other chair had books in it, so he sat down on Henry's bed.

"Last night I had dinner with Randal Chillingham." His blank look seemed to annoy her, and she added impatiently: "The producer, darling. He put on the Tchekov season last year, and now he's running the new theatre in the Haymarket. He's going to be a very important person."

"Is he a short darkish fellow, rather heavy in the shoulders?"

Cressida looked up curiously.

"Yes. Do you know him?"

"I only saw him once, that's all. It doesn't matter. Go on about the dinner."

"It was a very good dinner," said Cressida, still looking at him.

"I should hope so. Did he offer you a part?"

"Not exactly. You see . . ."

A new, an all-explanatory idea suddenly illumined Alistair's misery.

"Was he beastly to you? Shall I go and kick him?" But that made her smile, and he was reminded of the day in Kensington Gardens when she had stood so quietly with her hand in his. Her eyes, as then, were full of a grave experience; they looked at him coolly, impersonally; they made him feel very young.

"No. Don't kick him. It wouldn't do any good."

"Tell me what happened."

"We had dinner—"

"Where? At his place?"

"No, at the Ivy. But we went back. afterwards because he wanted me to read the part. It's a very good part." She paused, twisting and untwisting her fingers through the loop of her bag. "He liked my reading of it. And he said he'd give it me if . . ."

"Yes?" said Alistair.

She got up and walked over to the hearth. The mantel was covered with a fine grey film, and she drew a long wavering line with her forefinger. She said: "Your mantelpiece wants dusting."

Alistair waited. She was wearing a long black dress, very like the one in which he had first seen her, but with two narrow bands of white fur instead of the ruffles. It made her look even more slender than usual. "I suppose he's in love with you," said Alistair at last.

"I'm sorry, darling."

"The swine," said Alistair.

He crossed the room in three strides, fully determined to take her in his arms and comfort her; but something in her strange immobility checked him. Besides, why that odd little apology? It wasn't her fault if managers lost their heads—hardly theirs even, poor devils. A new thought struck him.

"Did you tell him you were engaged to me?"

Cressida smiled again.

"Of course, darling. But I'm afraid he hasn't been very well brought up."

"Don't laugh at me," said Alistair.

He was now standing as still as she, frozen to the heart by a great bewilderment. He didn't understand. Suddenly Cressida turned towards him, impatiently.

"You may call me what you like, my dear. I'm taking the part."

His mind must have been as numb as his heart, for even so it was several moments before he grasped her full meaning. Then, when the drumming of the blood was somewhat quieted, he moistened his lips and said dully, staring at the floor: "I suppose you're going to marry this fellow?"

She spared him.

"Yes."

"Do you care for him at all?"

"I don't dislike him. But—oh, don't you understand?—I can't wait any longer."

He understood. How could she be expected to wait, she so swift and beautiful and impatient? How could he have hoped to keep her, after the first days of spring? And yet, in some obscure way, he thought he would have minded less if she had been really fond of the fellow.

"You didn't love me either," he said unhappily.

"Alistair!"

The beautiful voice was scarcely more than a whisper. He thought how it would wring the hearts of the dress circle.

"And after all, why should you?" he reasoned. "I've often wondered what you could see in me. I've never quite been able to believe it."

A slim white hand—saint's hand, Cressida's hand—fluttered into his range of vision. He took it quickly and pressed it to his lips.

"Where's your coat?"

He found it tossed on to the table, and a little black hat trimmed with three tails of ermine. No one would ever wear such beautiful clothes as Cressida. She put them on carefully, even remembering to redden her lips at the glass.

"Good-by, Cressida."

"Good-by, my dear."

Good-by, Cressida. . . .

II

Alistair went over to the window. It was only about half-past six, too early to go to bed. He looked at the chair where Cressida had been sitting and thought how she would never sit there again. The dust on the mantel was marked by her finger: tomorrow morning Mrs. Griffin would wipe away dust and mark together.

"Cressida," he said aloud.

The quiet room had no comfort for him. It had so few memories of her that they were all poisoned by this last terrible hour: it could tell him nothing save that Cressida was false.

"That fellow," said Alistair.

Involuntarily he shut his eyes. It was no use blaming her; perhaps being like that was part of her, she couldn't help it. But it did seem hard on him, when he loved her so badly. Cressida, Cressida. . . .

Stiffly, like a man who has been sitting in the cold, he went and wiped the dust from the mantel and straightened the cushions in the chair. Then he turned back to the street, so bright by contrast with the darkening room that it seemed for a moment as though daylight had come flooding back like the last wave of an ebb-tide. The chimneys of the houses over the way stood out with exquisite precision against a violet sky: half-way down the road a man walked sharply outlined as a figure in an etching. It was intolerable. Alistair put his head down in his hands and gave himself up to grief.

CHAPTER XXIV

I

ESCAPING through the front gate Winnie heard some one call her name from down the road. It sounded like Eddie Cribb, but quickening her pace almost to a run she was round the corner and into Kimberly Street before he could come up with her. Here she jumped on to a 'bus (she was still fortunately carrying her bag), and took a ticket to Victoria; but the commiserating or curious glances (for the tears were still running down her cheeks) were too much for her, and at Marble Arch Winnie descended and continued her flight on foot.

Dusk had shut down on Oxford Street in a light spring mist, blurring all outlines to a melancholy vagueness. One or two shops were still open, but their windows had a deserted look. It was no weather for loitering, and as Winnie half walked, half ran over the empty pavement she felt as though she were the only soul left in a dead city. All the others— the rare passers-by, the huge looming policemen—were no more than ambulant shadows: as to them her own light scurrying figure was perhaps no more than an unlaid ghost.

It was nice to be able to cry without people bothering you. Winnie's tears were now falling more quietly, curiously hot against her mist-cold cheek, and now and then running into her mouth with a not unpleasant taste of salt. On several occasions she narrowly escaped being run over, particularly at one-way crossings; but the gods who care for the afflicted guided her steps and brought her in safety in Oxford Circus.

Here she hesitated, and finally turned right along Regent Street. Just before Piccadilly, however, she turned again, this time to the left, and presently found herself in a tangle of streets verging on Soho. She had not the least idea where she was going, being only anxious to drug her brain with rapid and incessant motion; but after a while, and somewhat to her surprise, she began to be conscious of a growing fatigue. A day behind the counter had left her in no trim for urban rambles at four miles an hour, and she wanted, quite simply, to sit down.

Reluctantly prepared to pay, if need be, as much as one-and-four, Winnie therefore began to look for a picture-house, but as luck would have it not one was to be seen; and turning down a likely side-street she found herself walking along beside the railings of a tiny churchyard.

Nothing can better illustrate her frame of mind than the fact that she at once stopped and had a look at it. A church! They always let you into churches, it was the Law, and you could sit down as long as you liked. But still Winnie hesitated. Perhaps it wasn't any one who could go in, only the regulars: and she herself hadn't been to church not since she was a kid. Suppose they turned her out?

"Coo, I'll just go quietly, that's all," thought Winnie; and turning in at the gate advanced boldly up the path. The door was open, and here she paused again, peering up the darkened aisle. The least rebuff and she would have turned tail; but the place seemed to be quite empty. Still half expecting to be ordered out, Winnie plucked up her courage and entered one of the pews. The bare wood felt very hard and cold, and she noticed with regret that some of the other seats had thick red cushions; but to change places merely for the sake of comfort seemed somehow irreverent, and she stayed where she was. After all, you didn't come to church to be comfortable.

You came to pray.

A trifle self-consciously Winnie slipped on to her knees.

"O Lord, I never was much of a one to go to church," prayed Winnie. "Not that I s'pose you've noticed anyway. . . ." She stopped, vaguely troubled by the informality of her tone. A distant echo of Sunday School prompted her to change to the second person singular. "O Lord, if it's not asking too much of Thee, make me not so unhappy. Truly, O Lord, if I don't feel better soon, I don't see how I can go on being like I always am, and Ma's ever so fond of me, truly she is. It's Arnold and Nina, O Lord . . ."

Again Winnie came to a halt. It seemed somehow mean to tell the Lord about Arnold and Nina, apart from the fact that He probably knew already; and as for praying any more on her own account, this struck Winnie as altogether too presumptuous. So closing her eyes tightly for the last time, she added the only petition that seemed at all important—"O Lord, please help Nina and Arnold"—and left it at that.

She then sat up again and waited for the answer.

It was not in her essentially modest nature to expect a private miracle—three pound notes, for instance, dropping out of a prayer-book: but she did anticipate a mild inner glow, a slight uplifting of the heart, some unostentatious sign that her prayer had been heard and noted. After ten minutes, however, she was conscious of no change save an increasing chilliness of hands and feet. Churches were nearly always cold, naturally; you couldn't expect them to be kept warm every day just on the off-chance that some one might want to come in; but Winnie was no polar bear to be converted on an iceberg. Soon she was shivering lamentably, and still no mystic warmth kindled in her breast. Instead, the awful blank despair, which she had a little shaken off, returned with new force. Worst of all, memories of Arnold, hitherto kept at bay by brisk movement, now came crowding back unchecked; and before the image of the baker's shop Winnie admitted defeat. The experiment had failed.

Without the least resentment she raised herself to her feet and bobbed stiffly towards the altar. There had been an R.C. kid at school who always did that, and Winnie had thought it ever so nice and respectful. The R.C. kid would have got an answer, you bet.

"I shouldn't be surprised if I wasn't a Christian at all," thought Winnie mournfully; and pulling up her collar with stiff fingers she carried her burden back into the street.

Once more in search of a movie-house, she struck left, and this time emerged into the misty brightness of Leicester Square. There were cinemas there right enough, ever such big ones, but her heart sank as she saw the queues waiting for the cheap seats. It was three-and-six before you could go straight in, and in spite of her weariness she wasn't that bad. Winnie pulled herself together and crossed the Square, looking out now for somewhere like the Riviera. The mist had turned to a fine rain, making her anxious for her hat, and she stepped into a doorway to have a look at it. The quill seemed to be all right, standing up as stiff as anything, so she put it on again and adjusted the angle in the shop window. It was a billiard-table shop, ever so big and fine, and from a notice inside she learned that there was a match going on that very moment.

"Charlie'd like that," she thought absently.

Then a thought struck her, and with sudden interest she turned back and looked at the price of seats. The cheapest was two-and-four—an awful lot, though better than the pictures; but she had to sit down somewhere, and there was a whole week's money in the pocket of her bag. Winnie stumbled up the stairs and bought a ticket.

Just inside the door two or three men stood blocking up the way, though from the click of billiard balls she knew the game must have begun. Normally Winnie would have dug her elbow into the nearest ribs and pushed through; but melancholy still had her in its grip and she waited patiently until, for no apparent reason, they all moved in together. The man immediately in front of her went and sat down in the second row, but Winnie had just sufficient presence of mind to notice that he was wearing evening dress, and attached herself instead to a youth in a light cloth cap. Under his unwitting guidance she mounted a flight of stairs and sat down with her back against the wall. It was ever so dark up there, and no one took any notice of you. Not if you cried quite quietly they didn't. . . .

So for half an hour or so Winnie cried very quietly indeed, wiping away the tears as fast as they fell, and never blowing her nose save under cover of an even louder blast from an old gentleman farther along. Gradually, however, the intense decorum of the atmosphere, coupled with a slight over-heating, began to exert its soothing influence. Winnie's tears ceased to flow, the old gentleman's trumpetings became a matter of indifference; and she was presently able to look up and take a feeble interest in her surroundings.

That it wasn't half dark had been, and remained, her dominant impression; but she now perceived the table itself, a long way below, to be as brilliantly lighted as a race track. (With a sudden jerk of the memory she recollected an appointment to go with Eddie to the dogs that very evening. No wonder he'd shouted after her. . . .) Under this concentrated radiance the green cloth showed smooth as smooth, making a fine background for the lovely red and white balls. Round this arena walked two players, both in their shirtsleeves; they hit not alternately, but ever so many goes at a time, and the balls ran about the table and dropped into the pockets as neat as anything. Winnie liked to see them do this, and to join in the subdued flutter of applause whenever (as she supposed) they had run about particularly well. A complete ignorance of the game—for though they went themselves Charlie and the boys would never take her to the Blue Lion billiard saloon—made it impossible for her to appreciate the finer points; but she was soon, in a quiet sort of way, enjoying herself very much indeed.

Extremely sensitive to atmosphere, Winnie found the peaceful dignity of the proceedings inexpressibly comforting. The religious silence of the congregation, the low, unvarying voice of the marker, the quiet, desultory click as of a sluggish hermit telling his beads—all combined to produce a feeling of almost holy calm. Happily responsive, she folded her hands in her lap and surrendered herself to the benign influence. It was the negation of passion.

Poor old Arnold. For the first time she was able to think of him without starting to cry. Poor old Arnold, he couldn't get much fun out of life. Nothing but politics and meetings. . . . You couldn't expect him to keep off the girls as well, it wasn't nature. Only living in the same house it was queer he never even . . .

"Oh, well, there's no accounting for tastes," reflected Winnie philosophically. It wasn't as though she hadn't enough boys already, and the thought of her eighteen Christmas presents (one or two of which must have cost at least five shillings) was a salve for any self-esteem. Arnold, *he* hadn't given her anything, he hadn't enough gumption; and she only hoped that girl would just take him in hand. Poor Arnold, he'd got a lot to learn.

Here Winnie broke off her train of thought to join in a burst of decorous clapping, and thus became conscious of her tear-soaked handkerchief, still rolled in a tight ball. She spread it out over the arm of the next seat, fortunately unoccupied, to give it a chance to dry.

From Arnold her thoughts now shifted to Nina. It was still difficult to realize that she had gone for good. The matter of the three pounds Winnie's mind had already glossed over (probably during the first desolate half-hour) by choosing to regard it as a temporary loan. The whole essence of a loan, reasoned Winnie's mind, was not whether you knew she was going to take it, but whether you knew she was going to pay back; and by this time it was so certain that she would that there was no need to consider the matter further. There remained, therefore, only an uncomplicated grief at the loss of her girlfriend, the sort of grief it would take a long time to get over, but which didn't really hurt like—like it might have done. And if you looked at it one way it was ever so thoughtful of Nina to go off like that and save her all the pain of saying good-by: because she hated partings, they made her feel blue as blue.

Almost cheerful again, Winnie opened her bag, and began powdering her nose. She didn't half look a mess, all that eyelash stuff in sooty streaks. Fortunately the handkerchief was still fairly damp, and with this she now cleaned off most of the black and corrected the outline of her drooping mouth. The result was paler than usual, but quite passable, and she was just preparing to give her whole attention to the game when every one suddenly got up and began to go. The show was over.

Surprised but docile, Winnie gathered up her possessions and followed the crowd. On the outer staircase she was jostled by a youth of prepossessing appearance, whom she told off with almost her usual gusto. He then invited her to accompany him to the Corner House, and on her refusing suggested an exchange of addresses. Winnie would have nothing to do with him, her mood, though lighter, being still far too chastened for casual flirtation; but the incident naturally did her good, and once safely on a 'bus she had no hesitation in waving violently.

"Oh, well, I'm not dead yet," thought Winnie; and with practically no effort she gave the conductor the glad eye.

II

Returning at last down Kimberly Street she became conscious of extreme hunger, and discovered, upon reflection, that she had not eaten since noon. Fortunately there was plenty of money in her bag, and circumstances seemed to indicate a blow-out; so instead of proceeding directly to Number Fifteen she stopped at the corner and turned into the Riviera. Owing to the lateness of the hour all the tables were empty except one, at which Charlie Coe sat reading the evening paper.

"Hello," he said, "where's the coat?"

"I didn't get it after all," replied Winnie carelessly, dropping into a chair and taking off her hat. "I've been seeing Nina off at the station."

"Nina?" Charlie looked up in surprise. "I thought she was staying with you for good and always. Have you had a row?"

"'Course we haven't. But she got a letter from her sister-in-law saying she could stay down there for a bit, so of course she went. What've they got tonight that's filling?"

"Roast beef and Yorkshire," replied Charlie promptly. "I had it myself, and that's why I'm here now." He pushed over the menu, watching her small dirty face as she tilted it to the light. It struck him that she looked disappointed about something.

"Feeling bad about that coat, kid?" he asked tactfully. "You'd fairly set your heart on it, hadn't you?"

"Well, and can't I change my mind if I want to?" snapped Winnie. "It had moth in the collar."

CHAPTER XXV

I

RETURNING rather earlier than usual from a visit to Pooh's flat, Henry was surprised to see no light in the top-floor windows; for Alistair had said nothing about being out, and it was long before his usual bedtime. The top landing, too, was in darkness, and Henry prepared to light the gas before going into the room. By this simple precaution he was able to avoid falling over the furniture, whereas Alistair always went blundering ahead and barked his shins.

On this occasion, however, he had run out of matches, and was consequently forced to adopt the more common procedure of groping to the mantel. He could just make out the dark bulk of the easy chair, and reaching out to it with the instinctive gesture of a man in the dark, his hand came in contact with some one's face.

In one and the same instant (or so it seemed) he was engulfed by terror and realized that there was nothing to be afraid of. It was Alistair, of course, who had fallen asleep over a book, before it was time to light up. Henry's hand slid down to his friend's shoulder and shook it.

"Alistair!" he said, a trifle louder than was necessary. "Wake up, old man!"

The figure stirred. Henry shook him again, apprehension—no terror this time, but a reasonable anxiety—suddenly renewed.

"Alistair, old man! Are you all right?"

Under his hand he felt the shoulder stiffen, and for an instant knew that the whole body had gone perfectly rigid. Then the tension relaxed, and Alistair's voice said slowly:

"What time is it?"

"Just after eleven. You've been asleep."

"Yes." The voice appeared to consider this explanation and decide that it would do. "Yes. That's it. I've been to sleep."

"You don't sound a bit well," said Henry anxiously. "How have you been feeling all evening?"

"Fit—as—a—fiddle, thanks," drawled the voice.

Henry gave it up until he could see what he was doing, and moving over to the mantel began feeling about for the match-box. It was at the far end, and by the meager rattle seemed to be nearly empty.

"Henry."

He spun round, though the darkness rendered the action ineffective.

"Don't light the gas."

"But my dear fellow . . ." Genuinely alarmed, Henry slipped the matches into his pocket and returning to the chair took Alistair's hand in his own. It was dry, but quite cool. "You don't feel feverish to me," he said solicitously.

"I'm not. I've had the most awful headache, that's all, and my eyes hurt like hell." Alistair sat up and put his hand to his forehead. "I've taken so many aspirins I can hardly think. Am I talking all right?"

"You sound a bit odd," admitted Henry. He had no words to describe the effect of those first husky sentences drawling out of the dark.

"My voice sounds about a mile off, but I suppose that's the aspirin. Get to bed in the dark, there's a good chap, and I'll turn in too." There was a slight pause, followed by a swift intake of breath that might have been a suppressed chuckle. "You've done it before now, haven't you?"

Entirely reassured, Henry admitted the impeachment and began taking off his tie. With much creaking of basket-work Alistair hauled himself out of the chair, a long thin figure just visible in silhouette, and moved stiffly across to his bed. Though obviously much recovered, there was still something in the way he walked, something in the rigid set of his shoulders, that roused Henry to almost painful sympathy. He looked as though he'd had a bad time, poor devil....

They had just got into their beds when suddenly Henry bethought himself of an interesting piece of news picked up at the flat, and which he knew Alistair would be pleased to hear.

"By the way," he said softly, "you know Cressida Drury? The girl you thought read so well? Pooh tells me she's just got an awfully good engagement at that new theatre in the Haymarket. We ought to go and see her."

But Alistair must have gone straight to sleep, for he made no answer.

II

Everything passes. For two or three days Henry continued to address his friend in a slightly lowered voice, then recovered his usual heartiness as it were between one sentence and another. Alistair's headache—for his fiction, like that of St. Elizabeth, had been immediately substantiated—was over even sooner; and there now remained only the trouble with his heart.

It was pretty bad. It was not so bad that he could not sleep, but bad enough to destroy his appetite: and for the first time in months his living expenses dropped back to thirty shillings a week. It would have been bad enough to stop him working, had opportunity arisen, and did actually prevent his accompanying Henry to an end-of-term dinner and dance. There were also moments when the agony of his loss was so great that he could hardly keep from crying aloud.

It was pretty bad on the light evenings, when every itinerant musician played *O Sole Mio!* and the pigeons began to coo in Bloom Street. It was pretty bad when Henry and Pamela took half an hour to say good night on the stairs. Perhaps it was worst of all when he saw the picture of Cressida on the back of a man's paper in the Underground. He could not read what it said underneath, probably something about the new theatre.

But everything passes, and little by little his interest in life began to return. It took the insidious form of complete indifference, and thus making its way past every barrier set Alistair seriously thinking what he should do next. It struck him, for instance, that his life, of no more use to himself, might just as well be devoted to the service of others, and within a fortnight or so he had begun to spend a good deal of time considering the relative merits of Dockland Settlements, Foreign Missions, and Boys' Clubs. Not one of them, however, seemed quite to meet the case.

He wanted something more individual. He wanted to do good not so much to a whole class of persons as to one single person, from whom he would in turn receive a passionate and personal gratitude. He also decided, while thus narrowing the field of his benevolence, that it would make things more interesting if the recipient were of the opposite sex. At which point, with all the a propos of a heavenly reward, Alistair received a remarkable inspiration.

He would marry Winnie Parker and take her away from it all.

Unlike most gift-horses, the idea seemed to Alistair to bear the closest inspection. It combined self-sacrifice, new interests, and immediate action. He saw himself at once correcting Winnie's pronunciation and encouraging her to read Lytton Strachey. His own work, too, would inevitably benefit, for even were he to flag under the spur of responsibility there would always be the gentler stimulus of constant admiration. Literary criticism, thought Alistair, would be a good line to take up: one had something to work on. And Winnie could verify quotations for him, and copy out his rough notes. . . . The memory of her really appalling scrawl bothered him a moment, until he remembered that besides taking writing lessons she could also learn to type. . . .

The exact moment of inspiration occurred about half-past twelve of a Saturday morning, in the middle of putting on his outdoor shoes; and having thoroughly considered its many advantages (the chief of which have just been recorded), Alistair came to the conclusion that there was nothing whatever to wait for. Immediate action being precisely what he needed, he determined to make a formal declaration that very afternoon, and with this object in view at once resumed the lacing of his shoes.

But his fertile meditations, though brief enough in abstract, had taken time, and Alistair now discovered that is was nearly three o'clock. It also occurred to him that he had had no lunch, and though not actually very hungry he still had sufficient sense to reject the idea of proposing on an empty stomach. A sort of prescient sheepishness, however, kept him away from the Riviera, and after walking right down Kimberly Street he turned into a sandwich-bar near the Edgware Road. At that time of the afternoon it was quite deserted save for a ginger cat and the lad behind the counter.

"Hello," he said cordially. "I thought we was never going to see you."

Alistair looked and saw that it was Sid Mason.

"Winnie sent you for one of our crab specials?" continued Mr. Mason, dusting a high stool with his own hands.

But Alistair refused this exotic delicacy, and ordered instead a ham roll and black coffee.

"Well, you know best," said Mr. Mason, with a prodigious and Rabelaisian wink. "Can't say I ever eat fish myself, not on a Saturday afternoon."

CHAPTER XXVI

I

HALF-an-hour later Alistair stood outside the Parker sitting-room, a prey to much the same sensations (only fortunately he did not remember them) as had once assailed him on Cressida's door-step.

"Come in!" cried Winnie.

Alistair opened the door, and by a rare stroke of luck found her quite alone. She was sitting on the edge of the table, polishing her nails, and for a moment he stood silent, trying to visualize her as the charming and cultured wife of a distinguished critic; but unfortunately she had put on even more make-up than usual, and the effort was very great.

"Well, d'you like what you're looking at?" inquired Winnie brightly.

But that was an opening for Charlie, or one of the boys—not for Alistair. However he advanced hardily enough and sat down beside her on the edge of the table. In normal circumstances each would have at once noticed, and commented on, the other's air of fatigue, but the coincidence of their distress made them unobservant. For some minutes they sat in complete silence, thinking respectively of Arnold and Cressida; then Alistair pulled himself together and said:

"Did you get your coat?"

The opening seemed to him rather well chosen, showing a sympathetic interest in her most trivial affairs; but to his surprise she merely remarked tartly that she hadn't known he was going to pay for it.

"I'm sorry," said Alistair. A bolder spirit might have found room, despite the tartness, for a neat *rélique*; he personally was not feeling bold at all. In order to ease the undoubted tension he extracted and lit one of Henry's French cigarettes, sending a gust of smoke wreathing between them.

"Don't mind me," said Winnie.

Alistair apologized again. It was plain that he had come at an unpropitious moment, but on the other hand the rare privacy which they now enjoyed was too precious to waste. Extinguishing his cigarette, therefore, he threw the stub into the grate and tried again.

"How's the shop?"

It was a particularly cunning question, designed to introduce a general discussion of her future, and he very much wished she would stop polishing her nails.

"Oh, not so dusty," said Winnie. "Makes you a bit tired, all that standing, but it's fun seeing the people. I'd rather be there than in a noffice any day. There's more life."

"But all the same," prompted Alistair, "you don't want to stay there for ever, do you?"

"Ooh, I dunno." She breathed loudly and exchanged the buffer for a piece of chamois leather. "I did used to think about getting into one of the big places, in Oxford Street, but it's ever so difficult. The girls are that smart you wouldn't believe, with lahdidah voices and everything. I'd be afraid to open me mouth."

"Nonsense," said Alistair, "your voice is very nice indeed." (He was quite right, Winnie's shrill pipe was as sweet as an oaten whistle.) "You only want a lesson or two to speak perfectly."

"Like you an' Mr. Brough, I s'pose," said Winnie. "Thawnks most awf'ly, but I reahly ahm most fratefully busy, most awf'ly decent of you I'm shaw."

Alistair, who had just been about to offer his services as a tutor, flushed brightly and refrained. The imitation, though ridiculously exaggerated, was just good enough to be embarrassing, especially as it seemed very unlikely that she should have been keeping the accomplishment to herself.

And yet—how quick and adaptable it proved her! She might jeer and parody, but the very parody showed his judgment to be correct. Inside six months the only perceptible difference between Winnie and Eeyore would be the former's superior charm and intelligence. She would never, for instance, make him look a fool by adoring in public. . . .

Nor in private either, most likely. The thought came pat as one of her own repartees, but without in the least affecting his resolution. After all, it wasn't for his own pleasure that he was marrying.

"Don't you ever take any one seriously?" he asked.

"Not often," said Winnie, bending so earnestly over her manicure that a frizz of fair hair fell into her eyes. She pushed it back behind one ear, thus revealing a new and totally unexpected profile, for by covering cheek and forehead with a mass of crimping Winnie effectually concealed her greatest beauty. The line from ear to chin was exceptionally pure, the temples and cheek-bones modelled with such delicacy that Alistair was reminded of the faces in the Primavera. For the first time emotion touched him, and he said:

"Take me seriously now, then. I—I want to ask you something."

"Go right ahead," said Winnie agreeably.

"Winnie—"

She looked up, tossing her hair free again.

"I—I want you to marry me."

The effect of his proposal left nothing to be desired. For a long minute Winnie sat perfectly still, the gap between her brightly-painted lips growing slowly wider and wider, the blue saucer eyes stretched to their fullest extent; but behind that startled mask, and even as she stared, her shrewd Cockney mind was already at work. In another moment it would have come to a conclusion, and Alistair watched, with an unexpected anxiety, the sudden lifting of her pointed chin.

"Garn," said Winnie.

Alistair stood up. Although more or less familiar with her vocabulary, the reply was not what he had anticipated. And indeed, Winnie herself seemed to feel that she had been a trifle abrupt, for the next moment she put out a skinny little paw and drew him back to the table.

"Don't be snorty," she urged. "I didn't mean to answer so short, it just slipped out. I thought you was having me on."

"I'm not, Winnie, I swear it," said Alistair. "I've never been more serious in my life."

"Oh!" She glanced curiously at his flushed and earnest face, and as though impelled by some queer modesty, quickly averted her gaze. The seconds slid by until it seemed as though neither of them was ever going to speak again. Then Winnie looked up and said slowly:

"What about your other young lady?"

"That's all over."

"Oh!" said Winnie again. There was a genuine sympathy in her voice, but also a certain satisfaction, as though she had just been enlightened on some difficult point. "I'm ever so sorry. It makes you feel bad, doesn't it?"

"It did at the moment," said Alistair, "but that's all over too." Even as he spoke enough of the agony returned to whiten his knuckles, but Winnie had returned to the polishing of her nails, and he was able to recover himself unperceived. "It's you now, Winnie. I—I don't want to do anything in the world except make you happy. I wish you'd give me a chance."

"Here, don't go on like that!" cried Winnie sharply.

"You're making me feel real bad." Though implicit, the refusal was beyond mistake, and with intense surprise he saw that there were two tears trickling down her cheeks. She took out a crumpled handkerchief and dried them carefully, so as not to smear her rouge.

"You see, you do like me a little," said Alistair.

"O' course I do. I think you're ever so nice."

"Then why won't you marry me?"

With an air of putting aside all sentiment, Winnie now considered the question from every possible angle. It did not take her long.

"What would we live on?" she asked.

That was a harder problem, and seconds ticked by while Alistair considered his various holds on fortune. At last he said (and it was the measure of his new sincerity):

"I expect I could get another teaching job."

"Mr. Brough says it's ever so difficult," observed Winnie.

Honesty compelled him to agree. It *was* difficult, even with a degree and training, and in his heart of hearts he knew that if he had wanted to go on teaching he should never have left St. Cuthbert's.

"You *are* a queer boy," said Winnie suddenly.

He turned his head, and found her big eyes fixed on him in the oddest mixture of wonder and compassion; and for the first and only time he caught a curious, fleeting resemblance to Cressida. It lay certainly not in feature, scarcely in expression; could be defined, indeed, only in terms of emotion; but somehow they both seemed very much older than he was.

"It's not real, you know," said Winnie gently. "Not like— like going to the shop. Just now you've got some idea in your head, and you think you want to marry me: but it's only your cleverness. You'll see, in a day or two you'll think of something else instead, and be as right as rain." She paused, and moved a little towards him. "But I'm ever so grateful to you, truly I am. You've helped me ever so."

"Have I really?" asked Alistair. That had been his intention, of course, but he did not remember having actually done so.

She nodded.

"Yes. When you came in just now I was feeling so bad I thought nothing mattered any more. I'd had enough of it, I just wanted to be dead. It didn't seem to matter what I did, nothing could make any difference. You know how you get sometimes?" She smiled, though wanly, and Alistair nodded. It was curious to hear his own train of reasoning so accurately reproduced. "Then you came in and—and asked me to marry you; and then I knew I wasn't bad enough to do a thing like that."

He was speechless.

"So you see, I'll always be grateful, won't I?" continued Winnie. "An' it's a lesson to me in a way, because when nothing happened at once I'd given up expecting. It just shows how right they are about having faith and not trying to hurry Him."

But Alistair did not hear her. It is doubtful, in any case, whether he would have been much edified. He was thinking over and over again the same phrase. He was thinking, "My God, that's damned funny!" Winnie saw and misinterpreted the twisted smile. Very gently she touched his arm, and said:

"We shouldn't have suited, you know. We're not the same class, to start with, let alone you being so much cleverer. Why, half the books and things you talk about I've never heard of. You've had education." Alistair looked doubtful. Life was not really so much easier to the educated as people seemed to imagine.

"I don't know," he said at last. "Being able to talk about books isn't everything. I may have had more education, but I shouldn't be a bit surprised if you had more sense."

"Why, I should hope so!" said Winnie blankly.

II

Upstairs he found Henry standing in an attitude of uncertainty before the Primavera. The amiable Mrs. Griffin had lent him an instrument for removing carpet-tacks, and he naturally wanted to get as much use out of it as possible. The Botticelli, however, belonged to Alistair.

"What about it?" he said. "Shall I have it down now, or do you want it left up till the last? It wouldn't take me a second with this jigger."

"It's got to come down some time, may as well be now," said Alistair. He felt too indifferent to mind, and Henry might as well have his pleasure.

"I've asked Mr. Hickey," continued Henry, "if we can put a Carter Paterson card in his window, and he says it'll be quite all right. By the way, I suppose you don't yet know what day you're leaving?"

Alistair pushed a sheaf of papers back into the table drawer and picked up his hat.

"I'm going for a walk," he said. "I'll tell you when I come back."

III

At the end of an hour's tramping he came to rest by the balustrade overlooking the head of the Serpentine. It was an exceptionally fine day, with just enough wind to make the water sparkle: but the beauties of Nature said remarkably little to his troubled soul.

He was trying to find out what had gone wrong. Eight months ago, in Stanley Avenue, the question would not have cost him a moment's thought. It was only too obvious what was wrong—Norbury, St. Cuthbert's, Aunt Gertrude objecting to a fire in his bedroom. No one could have created under those conditions; the whole atmosphere was too antagonistic. In Bloom Street, on the other hand . . .

In Bloom Street it had been just as bad. With all day at his disposal, meal-times as irregular as inspiration, a novel and stimulating *milieu*, he had literally nothing to show for it. Unless it were possible that meals could be too irregular, a *milieu* too stimulating, there seemed to be no explanation.

"And it isn't that I haven't had luck," pursued Alistair.

With a desolate honesty he acknowledged the many favours he had received of fortune. The very first meeting with Miss Tibbald, for example, through whom, by way of the Embryo Club, he had made the acquaintance of Raymond Paget. And then the astounding fluke of Paget's running into him again on the steps of the Albert Memorial, and that amazing evening in Camilla Dane's dressing-room. . . . All leading to nothing.

"It must be something in me," he thought. "It's only when it comes to me, when I have to take over, that everything goes to pieces." His play, for instance—they had all said it was good, even Mr. Markham; and yet he hadn't been able to carry it through. Even Henry's Bloomsbury crowd did better than that; their poems were at least finished. "I've never finished anything," thought Alistair. The truth was very near now; he would soon have to face it, but for a moment longer the sun-warmed stone was friendly against his hands.

How often had he leant there, staring over the water, and dreaming in deathless prose! He had meant to describe the flight of sea-gulls so that dwellers in Central Australia should look up as at a rush of wings. . . .

"The whole truth of the matter," said Alistair to the Serpentine, "is that I can't write at all."

It was out. He had stopped pretending. He had nothing left in the world.

With the unerring instinct of the self-tormentor he returned to the night when he had walked the streets of London with Cressida by his side. Life had seemed to be opening out before him, beckoning him on; love and fame waited for him to stretch out his hand. He remembered the moment under the lamp-post, when they had stood and promised fellowship.

It had all meant nothing, of course.

He tried not to think any more. Thinking was a mistake. He just stood where he was, staring before him; and since there are few better comforters than lapping water he presently began to feel a little easier. A woman with a bag of crumbs came to feed the ducks. She looked as though she might be going to speak to him, so he moved away and crossed to the other side of the water, the side where the pheasant was. ("The sea-gulls are all gone," said Cressida.)

Here, behind some railings, a man was sweeping the cut grass, and it seemed natural to stop and watch him. When there was a sufficient pile he scooped it together between two pieces of board and put it into a basket.

Somewhere else in the gardens Alistair had seen the cart that would come to fetch it away, an odd, high-tilted affair drawn by a shaggy horse. The man swept and scooped with perfect indifference to his audience until the last basket was full and there was nothing more to do except wait for the cart. Then he pushed back his cap and said:

"Nice arternoon."

"Very nice," said Alistair. The good garden odour followed him as he walked away, bringing back all sorts of summer-evening recollections. It struck him that it was a long time since he had cut any one's grass.

IV

About an hour later Alistair was at the table in the top room writing one of his rare letters. Or rather meditating, for it was not yet begun. Time and again he brought pen to paper, only to draw back at the last moment. He looked round the apartment, melancholy with Henry's packing, and at the faded patch where they had pinned the Botticelli. All over.

With sudden resolution he drew the paper closer and began to write.

My dear Uncle Severus . . .

CHAPTER XXVII

I

Number Fifteen was genuinely sorry to hear of Alistair's departure, but not much surprised. Henry, too, whose astonishment he had rather dreaded, received the news without any loss of composure.

"I think it's a very good idea," he remarked, slapping his books together to get the dust out. "My father always says Clark and Bailey make the best account books on the market, and he ought to know."

Alistair received this information with phlegm, and began clearing out the table drawers.

"After all," continued Henry, who was evidently in a talkative mood, "you'd hardly have wanted to stay here by yourself, would you?"

"Why not? It's very comfortable," said Alistair pugnaciously.

"Oh, I don't know. Somehow I'd always assumed you were going to look for a job at the end of the year."

The statement was sufficiently arresting to bring Alistair to his feet.

"I don't understand. Why should you always *assume* I was going to look for a job?"

Henry slapped the covers of the last book and began to fit them in the bottom of his trunk.

"Oh, I don't know," he repeated. "It seemed the obvious thing to happen. I've had a year too, and I've enjoyed it no end."

"So that's how you look at it," said Alistair, suddenly outraged, "a year's holiday, a last run round the meadow before you're put to plow?"

"Something like that," agreed Henry placidly. "No responsibility—that sort of thing."

"But *I* didn't mean it like that!" cried Alistair. He sought desperately for words in which to explain the blasphemy of such an attitude, but as usual they eluded him. "Look here, Henry, that very first evening when I found you cutting the grass—you didn't feel like this then? You didn't think I was coming for a year's lark before I began to look for a proper job? Why, that's when I *was* starting my proper job, for the first time in my life, and you believed it as much as I did. Henry, what's *happened* to everything?"

"Personally," said Henry, "I'm a year older. So are you, if you'd only realize it."

"When did you stop believing in me?"

"My dear fellow, it wasn't you individually I stopped believing in, it was the whole fairy-story. Fame in a night, and all the rest of it. I simply realized that it didn't happen."

"It has to some people."

"But not to you," Henry pointed out. He wedged a French dictionary into the bottom layer, and started on a second. "Look at your play," he said, not unkindly, "you never mention it now, so I suppose it's fallen through; but just at the beginning I thought that might be going to come true, and honestly, old man, no one could have been more pleased than I was. Only you see it didn't. It wasn't *real*."

"That was my fault," said Alistair. "It would have been all right but for me." Deep in his heart he knew that Henry was wrong, as wrong as the man who should deny the buoyant properties of water because he and his friends were unable to swim. "If only I could have shown him," thought Alistair yearningly; and the bitterness of frustration welled within him. It would have needed so very little genius to do the trick. . . .

"Cheer up, old man," said Henry kindly. "It'll always be something to look back on."

Alistair thought of Cressida under the lamp-post, Cressida by the fountains, Cressida in that very room; and decided that Henry was perfectly right.

II

That evening after dinner Winnie got out her album and went upstairs to levy contributions. She found Alistair alone, his friend having gone a-courting, and at once offered to fetch up some of the boys: but he was in no mood for society and declined with thanks.

"You'll soon have to get another book," he observed, fluttering the multicoloured leaves in search of a blank, A queer anthology it was—gems of verse, jokes from the comic papers, freehand sketches of domestic animals, nearly all vulgar and nearly all signed in terms of burning affection. One or two of the contributions were quite familiar—the verse about the wedding-cake, for instance; but he was not allowed to browse at leisure.

"Go on, write something," urged Winnie. "I want to see what you put."

A sudden desire to distinguish himself came over Alistair, and he asked nonchalantly:

"Quotation or original?"

"Ooh—'riginal, please," said Winnie, visibly impressed. He took out his fountain-pen and wrote rapidly:

"There was a young person called Winnie,"

(she wriggled with delight)

"Whose heart was as gold as a guinea,"

("Whose legs were remarkably skinny," would have been a better line, but in *vers de societé* a lady's feelings take first place)

"But though many implored it,

She'd never award it,
This prudent young person called Winnie."

"Well, you *are* a one!" said Winnie admiringly. She took the book and read the imbecile lines through again, this time with a slight knitting of the brows. Something was troubling her.

"Did you know," she asked shyly, "that you'd got *Winnie* twice?"

Alistair explained that this was the original and classic form of Limerick, as invented by Mr. Lear.

"But I'll alter it if you like," he added; taking back the album scratched out the last line. It was a rash thing to do, since he had not thought of an alternative; but Apollo loves the brave, and in a very few seconds the fire descended:

"And kept it safe under her pinny."

he finished triumphantly; and looking up met Winnie's eyes round with admiration.

"Oh, I do think you're ever so clever," she said simply.

The tribute was so rare in one of her ribald disposition that for a moment he could think of no reply; so to fill up the gap he reached out and gave her bony paw a gentle squeeze. The action had the cart-before-horse result of producing a slight tenderness.

"I wish I weren't going," he sighed.

"So do I," said Winnie.

"I've been awfully happy here."

"It's been ever so nice having you."

He sighed again.

"But of course you can't stay here not for always," said Winnie practically.

Alistair looked at her in astonishment. That was just what Henry had been saying. And as to Henry, he replied:

"Why not? I'm very comfortable."

"Oh, I dare say, but you're a gentleman really," said Winnie. As far as she was concerned that seemed to settle the matter; but Alistair persisted:

"Are you thinking I ought to get a proper job?"

"Well, we all come to it in the end," she said gently. "Look at Arnold now—he's a Communist, but he has to work just the same as every one else."

"I see!" He released her hand. "You must think I've been wasting a good deal of time."

"Oh, well," said Winnie again, "you're ever so young really. . . ." She looked at him with great kindness, quite ready to part with a kiss if so requested; but he seemed to have gone queer. Maybe he had been a bit fond of her after all, she reflected interestedly, in which case they often wanted to be left alone; and after a few more expressions of sympathy Winnie took her album and went thoughtfully downstairs, feeling rather solemn and important, like when she went to see Reggie in hospital. . . .

Alistair pushed back his chair and went over to the hearth. There was still some gas in the meter, but they were saving it for tomorrow's breakfast, and he did not feel reckless enough to light the fire. Fortunately his dressing-gown was still unpacked, so he put it on and for the last time folded himself into the easy-chair. Except for an occasional creaking when he moved his knees the dismantled room was quite still.

They were all wrong. They were so wrong that they would never even begin to understand what he, Alistair, knew by instinct. The thought gave him a feeling of superiority that was at the same time curiously free from conceit. For though he knew, he could not explain; nor could he even act upon his knowledge. He thought:

"I'm just clever enough to know that creation is the only important thing on earth, and just not clever enough to create myself. Only it isn't exactly cleverness, either. ... But I thank God I'll never be happy with these damned account-books. I'd rather go unsatisfied all my days than be like Henry."

For a moment longer he stared proudly at the future. Then St. Peter's clock struck eleven, and as though he had been waiting for the signal Alistair got up and finished his packing.

III

The following morning Henry left immediately after breakfast, with the design of seeing Pamela off to Devonshire and possibly accompanying her a short portion of the way, so that Alistair was therefore left to make his way back to Norbury alone. Winnie and Charlie offered to go with him as far as Paddington; but he felt quite sincerely that this would be taking too much trouble, and refused with many expressions of esteem. They insisted, however, on carrying his bags as far as the 'bus stop.

"I hate people going away," said Winnie soberly. "It makes me blue as blue." Spoke with genuine feeling, so that both men were uneasily conscious that she might quite possibly be going to cry.

"Here, give him a chance," said Charlie. "The next thing you know you'll be having him back again. He's not dead yet."

"One thing I do know," added Alistair, "you'll have forgotten me long before I forget you. Here, what's that thing in your album?

> "Think of me on the river,
> Think of me on the lake,
> Think of me on your wedding-day,
> And send me a piece of cake!"

The doggerel, thus spoken aloud and in the open air, had never sounded more idiotic, but Winnie brightened considerably.

"You bet I will," she promised, "a good big bit too; I do think those little silver boxes are lovely!"

Over the top of her head Charlie Coe winked majestically, and for the last time Alistair reflected with amazement that this dignified youth could not be more than twenty. In poise and *savoir-fair* he could give points to Mr. Hickey himself.

"Here's your 'bus!" cried Winnie.

With a quite unnecessary expenditure of energy they signaled it to stop. Assisted by Charlie Alistair hauled his two suit-cases onto the platform and obtained the conductor's permission to leave them under the stairs. Then, just as the 'bus started, urged by a sudden impulse, he dropped back on to the step and said huskily:

"You—you've been awfully decent to me. I'm most frightfully grateful."

"Oh, get back into the oven!" cried Winnie Parker.

IV

As the 'bus slowed down to take the corner Alistair caught a last glimpse of the Madonna of the Shoe-shop. Above her head the heavy swags were flushed to crimson, for a specially cheap line of bedroom-slippers had just come in; but there was another and a greater difference for which he could not immediately account. The whole group had been in some way altered and enriched, and by more than a bright splash of colour. Alistair craned energetically, for the 'bus was already gathering speed; and at the last moment understood. Familiar against the Madonna's knee, reaching up to the Child's dimpled hands, now leant an Infant St. John.

"It's time I got on with things," thought young Alistair.

THE END

FURROWED MIDDLEBROW

Ingram Content Group UK Ltd.
Milton Keynes UK
UKHW041714250423
420754UK00001B/236

9 781913 527631